RUTH AND THE KING OF THE GIANTS

A SEVEN KINGDOMS TALE 5

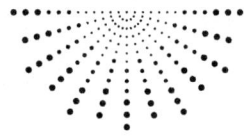

S.E. SMITH

ACKNOWLEDGMENTS

I would like to thank my husband Steve for believing in me and being proud enough of me to give me the courage to follow my dream. I would also like to give a special thank you to my sister and best friend, Linda, who not only encouraged me to write, but who also read the manuscript. Also to my other friends who believe in me: Julie, Jackie, Christel, Sally, Jolanda, Lisa, Laurelle, Debbie, and Narelle. The girls that keep me going!

And a special thanks to Paul Heitsch, David Brenin, Samantha Cook, Suzanne Elise Freeman, and PJ Ochlan – the awesome voices behind my audiobooks!

– S.E. Smith

Paranormal Romance
RUTH AND THE KING OF THE GIANTS: SEVEN KINGDOMS TALE BOOK 5
Copyright © 2019 by S.E. Smith
First E-Book Published September 2019
Cover Design by Melody Simmons

ALL RIGHTS RESERVED: This literary work may not be reproduced or transmitted in any form or by any means, including electronic or photographic reproduction, in whole or in part, without express written permission from the author.

All characters, places, and events in this book are fictitious or have been used fictitiously, and are not to be construed as real. Any resemblance to actual persons living or dead, actual events, locales, or organizations are strictly coincidental.

Summary: A human woman's determination to find her missing brother leads her to a magical world where giants live – and she finds love.

ISBN: (KDP Paperback) 9781688208254
ISBN: (BN Paperback) 9781078746939
ISBN: (eBook) 9781944125806

Romance (love, explicit sexual content) | Action/Adventure | Fantasy Dragons & Mythical Creatures | Contemporary | Paranormal (Magic)

Published by Montana Publishing, LLC
& SE Smith of Florida Inc. www.sesmithfl.com

CONTENTS

Prologue	1
Chapter 1	11
Chapter 2	23
Chapter 3	32
Chapter 4	43
Chapter 5	54
Chapter 6	61
Chapter 7	69
Chapter 8	74
Chapter 9	82
Chapter 10	93
Chapter 11	102
Chapter 12	111
Chapter 13	119
Chapter 14	125
Chapter 15	133
Chapter 16	143
Chapter 17	151
Chapter 18	156
Chapter 19	163
Chapter 20	171
Chapter 21	177
Chapter 22	185
Chapter 23	197
Chapter 24	205
Epilogue	214
Additional Books	223
About the Author	227

CAST OF CHARACTERS

Isle of the Giants: Kingdom of the Giants

Giants:

Koorgan: King of the Giants
Gant: Second-in-Command of the Giants
Edmond: Elder guard and Third-in-Command of the Giant palace guards
Hermon: giant – tends the magic mushrooms of the giants
Madura: half-witch/half giant: Spellbinder of the giants

Pirates:

Ashure Waves: King of the Pirates
Bleu LaBluff: Ashure's Second-in-Command of the Pirates and Captain of one of the Pirate Fleet
Dapier: Ashure's Head of Acquisitions for his ship

Humans:

Ruth Hallbrook: Forensic Accountant and sister of Mike Hallbrook
Mike Hallbrook: Detective with the Yachats Police Department and Ruth Hallbrook's brother
Tonya Maitland: human, Undercover investigative reporter pretending to be an FBI agent investigating the disappearances in Yachats, Oregon.
Asahi Tanaka: human, CIA Agent investigating the disappearances in Yachats, Oregon
Gabe Lightcloud married to Magna: human, works for the U.S. Fish and Wildlife collecting data.

Dr. Kane Field married to Magna: human doctor from Yachats, Oregon.
Carly Tate married to Drago: Banking Associate from Yachats, Oregon
Jenny Ackerly married to Orion: School Teacher and Carly's best friend
Ross Galloway: human, Fisherman from Yachats, Oregon

Seven Kingdom Characters:

Magna (Sea Witch) married to Gabe Lightcloud and Kane Field: half witch/half sea people. She is Orion's distant cousin on his father's side
Drago married to Carly Tate: King of the Dragons.
Orion married to Jenny Ackerly: King of the Isle of the Serpent (Merpeople)
Marina married to Mike Hallbrook: Witch
Magika: Queen of the Isle of Magic
Oray: King of the Isle of Magic
Nali: Empress of the Monsters

SYNOPSIS

The King of the Giants has met his match...

When her brother goes missing, Ruth Hallbrook follows the only lead that she has – a story told to her by a strange woman she meets in town. Armed with a 'magical' shell that will supposedly guide her, all she has to do is repeat the words she hears when she puts it to her ear. That would have been fine if she could have understood what it was saying! One wrong word lands her in a kingdom filled with giants, including one very large, irritating one who thinks she belongs in his gilded cage – fat chance of that!

An opportunity to escape for a little peace and quiet turns into a disaster when Koorgan, the King of the Giants, finds himself stuck in an old well. Unable to climb out, he is sure his only hope of rescue is the search party eventually finding him. The last thing he expects is his rescuer to be barely larger than his hand.

Afraid that something might happen to the tiny creature, he feels duty bound to help her find her missing brother and return her to her world. The trouble is, the more time he spends with her, the less he wants to let her go.

Life is dangerous on the Isle of Giants for the diminutive Ruth. It will take every skill this King of the Giants possesses to protect her. Guided by the legend of a mythical plant said to have created the giants, Koorgan will not rest until he finds a way to keep Ruth by his side. Find out if love can overcome the barrier created by a misspoken spell!

PROLOGUE

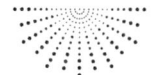

Six months before:

JFK Airport, New York City

"Damn it, sis! Don't you ever answer your phone? This is Mike. I wanted to let you know that I'm okay. Listen, something incredible has happened, but I wanted to let you know that I'm safe – and happy. Oh, Charlie is with me, so don't worry about the damn dog. I've met the most incredible woman. She's from another world, honest to god, she is. I know how that sounds, but I…"

Ruth Hallbrook muttered under her breath in frustration as her brother's message got crazier and crazier. He spun an incredibly detailed fairy tale that he seemed to whole-heartedly believe, and then the message abruptly ended mid-sentence.

Weaving in and out of the crowded airport terminal, she pressed the play button on her phone again and held her cell phone to her ear. Her purse strap started to slip and she had to lift her shoulder to keep it and her briefcase strap from falling off her shoulder – not an easy feat while she was pulling her carry-on behind her. She gritted her teeth when two young girls suddenly stopped in front of her and she almost ran into them.

"Watch out!" she barked out in a sharp voice.

The girls rolled their eyes at her as she passed them. Tension built in her when she realized she still had four more gates to go before she reached her destination. Fear, adrenaline, anger, and caffeine had been her constant companions for the past twelve hours.

She had been working overseas as a consultant for the last three and a half weeks and hadn't bothered with her personal cell phone once the battery died on it. She'd thought she had forgotten her charger, and since she and Mike only chatted once a month, she hadn't worried about her dead phone as she knew she would be back home before their next scheduled call. If something really important happened, Mike knew he could contact her on her work phone.

When she discovered that she had put it in a different zippered pocket of her suitcase, she had charged her phone this morning while frantically getting ready for the airport.

His message had been the last one in her voicemail. All the other messages had been spam except for the reminder that she had a dentist appointment coming up and the message from a man named Asahi Tanaka who claimed to be a CIA agent – a claim that a friend of a friend had verified for her. Unfortunately, the long line of messages had filled up her voicemail box, and the most important message of all was cut short.

"I swear if I get one more call about a new Visa, the IRS coming to lock me up, or my car warranty expiring, I'm going to reach through the phone, throttle the assholes on the other end, and tell them to get a real job!" she growled as she briskly walked through the JFK airport in New York.

She must have spoken a bit louder than she'd realized because several people turned to stare at her. They quickly turned their focus elsewhere when she shot them a heated glare. She glanced at the ticket in her hand. She had changed her New York to California connecting flight to Portland, Oregon instead so she could find out what in the hell was going on herself.

"This is so coming out of his Christmas present," she muttered as she pressed redial.

"Come on, Mike, pick up! You complain about me not answering the damn phone when you call," she muttered.

Ruth grimaced when she heard the last boarding call for her flight, followed by an announcement to her, Ruth Hallbrook, to please check in with an airline representative at the gate.

"What the fuck do you think I'm trying to do?" she crossly snapped.

She made it to the gate before they finished saying the message a second time. Gripping her phone in a white-knuckled grasp, she thrust her boarding pass at the gate attendant. The woman looked at her, opened her mouth, then closed it. Ruth knew exactly why – she looked like something the dog had not only dragged in, but had buried for a few days before digging it up.

That's what happens when you complete a month of long meetings, find out your frigging brother has disappeared not once, but twice, and discover that he left a cryptic message about an incredible woman from another world on the cell phone you had to turn off during takeoff. Then add in a flight halfway across the world. Mike's probably off to visit ET at Area 51, by now. He'll just traipse over to the bottom of Meteor Crater, except, oh wait, that's been moved to the Devil's Tower made out of mashed potatoes! she tiredly thought, realizing in that moment just how many weird movies she had watched.

An inelegant snort of laughter escaped her at the thought. The unexpected laughter caused the flight attendant standing in the door of the jet to give her a questioning look as she entered the plane. Shaking her head, Ruth passed the attendant and moved down the aisle to her seat. She stored her carry-on in the overhead compartment, tucked her briefcase under the seat in front of her, and sighed as she sank down into her seat in the First Class section.

She toed off her high heels, wiggled her toes, and fastened her seat belt. The man sitting in the window seat next to her looked vaguely familiar, but he just glanced at her and smiled before he went back to reading his newspaper. That suited Ruth just fine. She was in no mood to endure polite social interactions at the moment. She was too busy plotting where she was going to bury her brother's body.

Another tired sigh left her as the flight attendant began the safety presentation. She glanced at the headline of the newspaper the man was holding – 'Independent Audit Exposes Major Embezzlement in Largest On-line Retail Corporation'. Her lips curled into a menacing smile that made the flight attendant stammer over what to do if they had to make an emergency water landing before Ruth took pity on the woman, leaned her head back, and closed her eyes.

And people think the police have all the fun, she wearily thought.

She had been the lead forensic auditor on the case presented by the government, and the discrepancies she discovered had opened a can of worms that would keep fishermen supplied for centuries. That case had closed right before she left for Europe, but the trial hadn't started until yesterday. The case was a big reason why her most recent client had hired her. She was a brilliant detective when it came to numbers.

Her brother, on the other hand, was a great detective for the Yachats, Oregon Police department, which was why it was so strange for him to leave everything so abruptly to run off with some woman. He loved his job. He was good at it. That town needed him, and he knew it.

Still unable to sleep thirty minutes later, Ruth opened her eyes, turned on her phone, and scrolled through the automated text record of the message Mike had left her. *I've met the most incredible woman....*

When his department had informed her of his disappearance late last night, Ruth had demanded they send their entire case findings to her and keep her updated. One advantage to having friends in high places who hoped she would never thoroughly audit their finances was that when she asked for help, she was never denied.

Three hours in the Business Lounge at Heathrow had given her a chance to print out and read through the documents. She'd spent the flight to New York messaging back and forth with the Police Department, the FBI, and Agent Asahi Tanaka who had also emailed her.

Pursing her lips, she dragged her briefcase out from under the seat and removed the manila folder and a pen from inside the case. She pulled down the tray from the back of the seat in front of her, and opened the folder. Inside was her brother's banking and credit card information, and the reports and photos from the investigation to date. The most recent documents were the letters Mike had faxed right before her transatlantic flight had departed.

His office had sent her copies of his letter of resignation and a report indicating that the missing persons' cases he had been working on had a happy ending. Jenny Ackerly and Carly Tate, the two missing women, were fine. They had just decided to leave as suddenly and inexplicably as he had, and had decided to stay off the grid while their loved ones worried – for years in Carly Tate's case. There was a smiling picture of them to prove it.

The most recent photos taken at Mike's home made it seem as if he'd left voluntarily. The lock wasn't picked, as far as the investigators could tell, and there were now pictures and clothes missing. Was she supposed to believe Mike thought he didn't need clothes when he first went missing, but now he did?

Something had happened in the brief time since she'd last talked to him. Mike's message would have her believe that he'd met a woman and just disappeared from the face of the Earth, leaving everything behind except his wallet, keys, phone, and his dog. Was Ruth the only one that thought something pretty damn, fucking weird was going on?

"Nothing – absolutely frigging nothing," she muttered under her breath as she stared at the statements. "No purchases, no withdrawals, no credit card usage," she fumed, doodling on the paper as she thought.

"Ma'am, your drink order?" the flight attendant asked.

Ruth glanced up at the woman looking expectantly at her, and Ruth realized that this must be the second time the flight attendant had asked the question.

"Bourbon on the rocks," she requested.

"Yes, ma'am. Would you like the chicken or salmon dinner?" the flight attendant continued.

"Chicken," Ruth distractedly replied, tapping the tip of the pen on the paper in front of her.

She returned her attention to the financial records in front of her. The flight attendant brought the drink that she had requested and Ruth gave a brief murmur of thanks. She sat back as the woman handed the man beside her his drink.

"A Bourbon Woman. I haven't met one of those in a while," the man sitting next to her commented with a flirty tone.

Either the guy is hard up or I don't look as bad as I thought I did – which is a shame because it would save him from being eaten alive – especially since I remember why he looks familiar now, she thought in resignation.

"I'm not surprised," she replied, her tone dismissive as she returned her attention to the folder.

"Are you having a little trouble balancing your bank account? My ex-wife thought if there are checks in the checkbook, there must be money in the bank. Women! I swear if you don't put them on an allowance, they wouldn't know what to do," the man chuckled.

Ruth stared at the back of the seat in front of her, her fingers curling around her pen with more force than necessary. She looked down at the paper and smiled when she saw that her doodling had produced a coffin with a stick figure of her brother trying to climb out of it.

Do not engage, Ruth, she told herself. *You have a long flight ahead. DO NOT ENGAGE.*

She knew that was a futile admonition, though. She relaxed her fingers on the pen, picked up her drink, and took a sip, her decision made. She already knew his name and more about his business than he'd like her to know, but more information was always a good thing.

Ruth studied him more closely. The suit and Italian shoes that he was wearing were expensive, but the Rolex watch on his wrist was a fake. He would have realized it if he had read the misspelling on the brand name inside the crystal – Rolex should have one 'L' not two. He also had the smell of alcohol on his breath before he ever took a sip of the drink that was delivered to him, which told her that he had been enjoying the First Class Lounge pre-flight.

"Why, bless your little heart, Mr....," Ruth began with a saccharine smile.

"James Hornet, but you can call me Jim, sweetheart," Jim replied with a self-assured smile.

"James Hornet...." Ruth tilted her head and looked at him with a feigned thoughtful expression. "You wouldn't happen to be *the* James Hornet of Hornet Communications? Didn't your company neglect to report a billion-dollar deal with a Taiwanese company with ties to China? That was quite an accounting error! It garnered you a ten million dollar fine and an investigation from the Department of Justice. I believe I read in the Financial Times that the deal in question ultimately fell through, but gosh, Hornet Communications would have been stuck with owing a total of, let me guess..." She tapped her pen for a second. "Twenty-five million, four hundred thirty-two dollars, and sixty-four cents? It would be rounded to the nearest dollar, of course. Fines, penalties, and legal fees really do add up, don't they? You aren't *that* James Hornet, are you?" she asked with an innocent smile.

The man paled and shook his head. "No... I... How could you...?" he sputtered, looking down at the file in front of her.

Ruth gave her best impression of the shark from Jaws about to devour the poor unsuspecting swimmer in the opening scene.

Never go swimming at night in shark infested waters and never piss off an accountant, she thought.

"I'm Ruth Hallbrook. I was the forensic auditor on your case last year for the Department of Justice – so thank you kindly for your concern, but I can balance a checking account just fine, Mr. Hornet. In fact, you could say 'right down to the last penny'," Ruth replied, watching the man grow even paler.

"My apologies, ma'am," he said stiffly.

God, I hope he doesn't have a heart attack. I do not want to have to sit next to a dead guy for the next seven hours, she thought.

"Excuse me. I need to go to the bathroom," he angrily muttered, his face flushed with color.

Ruth stood up and stepped to the side as Jim clumsily exited his seat. She sat down and picked up her folder. It wasn't long until she noticed Jim emphatically speaking to another flight attendant. Amusement and relief swept through her when they both glanced at her before the woman motioned toward the back of the plane. Jim nodded and hurried to the curtained area.

"Your dinner," the flight attendant proffered.

"Thank you," Ruth politely responded, ignoring the flight attendant when she tried to inconspicuously sniff Ruth as she leaned in and deposited the dinner on the tray.

"I'm a forensic accountant. I conducted the audit on his company. You can probably guess it didn't go very well for him," she murmured with a tired smile.

"Ah," the flight attendant responded with an apologetic look.

"Works every time," Ruth murmured.

"I hope you enjoy the rest of your flight, ma'am," the flight attendant replied with a grin.

"I'm sure I will – now," she answered.

Her stomach growled as the scent of the chicken and vegetables hit her.

She placed the file on the seat next to her, and slowly enjoyed her meal, her mind going back over everything she knew.

Everything will be alright, Ruth. You won't lose the only family you have left in the world, the only person who can put up with your sarcastic mouth. He's just…having a midlife crisis, that's all. Mike will open the door and have a container of his special spaghetti sauce and homemade ranch dressing waiting for you.

Seven hours later, she looked through the window as the plane landed at Portland International Airport in Oregon. The knot in her stomach had grown the closer she got to the west coast.

The moment the captain announced that cell phones could be used, she turned off airplane mode on her phone and impatiently waited for it to connect to the nearest cell tower. Her fingers trembled as she dialed her brother's number.

"This is Detective Mike Hallbrook. I'm either on another call or unable to take your call at the moment. Please leave a message and I'll get back with you."

"I'm sorry, the mailbox you are trying to reach is full," the automated voice replied after the beep.

Ruth took in a deep breath and looked out the window. Well, Mike always said that she had been born with a triple-dose of tenaciousness. He was about to find out she'd been born with a hell of a lot more than that!

"You, baby brother, have just been put on your big sister's shit list," she muttered under her breath, sliding her heels back on and gathering her personal belongings. "Ready or not, here I come!"

CHAPTER ONE

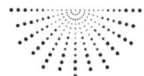

Present Day:

Seven Kingdoms: Isle of the Giants

"What has you so riled up?" Gant asked with a huge grin.

Koorgan shook his head and kept walking. As Gant followed him, his boots against the hard stone floors sounded like a herd of Nali's Hippogriffs charging down the hallway.

"Do you always walk this loud?" he growled.

Gant chuckled. "You've been doing paperwork again, haven't you?" he asked.

Koorgan winced when his friend, chief advisor, and Captain of the Guard slapped him on his shoulder. He resisted the urge to throw Gant out the window. The only reason he didn't was because there would more than likely be more paperwork involved in dealing with the cost of the replacement and repair to the window, and Gant would probably demand a few days off as compensation.

"Ashure sent another one of his contracts – and this one was especially... annoying," he replied with a sigh. He'd practically thrown Ashure's latest diplomat out and told the man to not come back. If Ashure wanted to do business with the Isle of Giants, he'd better start offering better deals. At this point, Koorgan was about ready to go stomp the arrogant pirate flat.

"Why don't you hire someone to take over the mundane stuff?" Gant suggested.

Koorgan stopped and turned to face Gant. "Don't you think I've tried? That damn pirate seduces every woman I've assigned – and before you ask, he didn't stop even when I put Agatha in charge! The woman has to be pushing five hundred years! She is a cyclops for crying out loud! If I put a man in charge, they are either too intimidated by Ashure or seduced by the jingle of gold. I would ban him if we didn't need his wares so badly. Negotiating so much with *him* is a steep price to pay for closing our borders," Koorgan grumbled. "I am starting to wonder if I would rather have dealt with the evil spreading through the kingdoms. Between that, the blight, the accounting, the inventory, the contracts, and dealing with other diplomats... I feel like I'm suffocating here. I hate it, Gant," Koorgan admitted.

Koorgan immediately felt bad for unloading on his confidant. Advising a king was no easy job, and Koorgan tried not to impose on Gant unnecessarily, afraid someday their friendship would break under the strain. He ran his hand down his face before dropping it to his side.

Gant gazed back at him with a serious expression. "I understand... and you know, your upcoming nuptials will help solve at least one of those problems. Perhaps we should speak of...?" Gant gingerly asked.

Koorgan shot Gant a hostile glare. "No," he growled, turning and starting to walk again.

"You do understand that it helps to have a woman – or man if that is what you want – already picked out *before* you contemplate marrying them, don't you?" Gant called out from behind him.

"Shut up, Gant! You are not helping me," Koorgan retorted.

Koorgan kept walking. He needed to get out for a while to clear his head. The guards standing by the main doors hurried to open them when they saw the dark scowl on his face. He swept through the doors and was down the steps by the time Gant caught up with him again.

"What was so annoying about Ashure's contract?" Gant inquired, keeping pace with him.

"He offered to find me a bride in exchange for a ton of trees and three barrels of my finest brandy," Koorgan replied.

Gant looked at him in surprise. "That doesn't sound like a bad offer. It would fulfill the requirements," he said.

Koorgan scowled. "I don't wish to allow anyone – much less that damn pirate – to pick out who I will take as my bride," he snapped.

Gant grabbed his arm and stopped him. Koorgan reluctantly turned to face his friend. He impatiently shrugged his arm free.

"You know what will happen if you don't find someone, Koorgan," Gant warned.

Koorgan felt the weight of his responsibility bearing down on his broad shoulders. Yes, he knew. The Kingdom of the Giants would be no more.

The Rule – the governing force set forth by the Goddess herself – stated that for the giants to find harmony, their leaders must find a mate who completed them by their two hundred and thirty-fifth year. If he or she did not, the last of the mushrooms that gave them their magic would die. The giants would be reduced to mere mortals, unable to defend themselves against the other kingdoms. Already a mushroom blight was spreading through their kingdom.

"The mushrooms have been disappearing faster than we can grow them, and the ones already harvested have begun to turn to ash," Koorgan said grimly.

Gant nodded. "I wish it were otherwise, my friend. Leading the search has been…a discouraging exercise," he told Koorgan.

"I still have a few more weeks before I need to make a decision. I'm going out for a little while," he said.

Gant looked doubtful before he nodded. "I ordered the new members of the guard to meet me in the courtyard for training, but if you can give me a few minutes to arrange for Edmond to take over, I'll ride with you," he said.

Koorgan shook his head. "No, keep your training session. I'll be back within the hour. I'm just going for a short ride. I need the time alone to clear my head," he said.

"If you are sure. Please stay close to the palace this time. Your short rides tend to leave me with ulcers. You have to remember, I've known you our entire lives. You have a bit of a knack for getting yourself into trouble," Gant replied, his forehead creased and his smile strained.

Koorgan chuckled. "There is no need to worry, my friend. We are no longer boys. I can take care of myself. I won't go far or be gone long. Besides, Genisus needs to stretch his legs. There isn't another steed in the Kingdom that can keep up with him. A few times around the field will be good for him," he replied, resting his hand on Gant's shoulder and squeezing it in reassurance. He knew Gant was as worried about him as he was about the kingdom. Koorgan wouldn't let his people down – even if it necessitated making a deal with a pirate.

The worst thing about the Rule was that he was required to choose a bride who was not from the Isle of the Giants. That limited his choices to a dragon, a mermaid, a witch, an Elemental, a pirate, or a monster – and there were a few problems with each of those options. The relationships between the Isle of Giants and the other Kingdoms were cordial, but there wasn't much trust shared.

He had resigned himself to the fact that his wife would likely be a spy for whichever Kingdom he picked, and he *had* looked for someone he could stand to share his life with, he really had, but…it wasn't like the aftermath of war was conducive to this sort of thing. The Isle of Magic was the most recent kingdom to have been devastated by the Sea Witch's treachery, but every kingdom was affected, and had been for a long time. He felt tired just thinking about it.

"Your mount is ready, Your Majesty," the stable boy said, holding the reins to a large steed who was pawing at the ground.

"Thank you," Koorgan replied.

Koorgan ran his hand along Genisus's muzzle before caressing the huge battle steed's jaw. The thick, coarse hair shimmered under his touch. He took the reins from the stable boy, gripped the saddle, and swung himself onto the stallion's back. The stable boy stumbled back when Genisus rose up on his hind legs, pawing the air, and tossed his head.

"Easy, boy. I know it has been a while since we've enjoyed a good ride. How about we remedy that?" Koorgan chuckled.

The stallion nodded his head vigorously in agreement. Koorgan's eyes glittered with excitement. He leaned forward and tapped his heels into Genisus's side.

The stallion bolted, the power in the huge body surging them forward with a flurry of flying dirt. Koorgan's laugh filled the air.

"Clear the gates!" a guard yelled.

The guards at the gate quickly ran to help those entering and exiting the palace clear a path. Koorgan raised a hand in thanks as Genisus and he flashed by. Residents of the Isle of Giants turned with smiles on their face as he raced by them.

Their trusting smiles added more weight to his shoulders. When Koorgan turned Genisus toward the vast forests, the stallion's muscles gathered and his hooves dug deeper into the soft soil beneath the grass as if Nali's monsters were nipping at their heels.

∼

Several hours later, Koorgan pulled Genisus to a halt. The stallion was nervously prancing and Koorgan could feel a shiver of tension run through the horse's body. He reached forward and patted the stallion's neck while he scanned the area.

Following the tracks of a wild boar, he had turned down a seldomly used trail that became narrower and narrower until it was barely more than a footpath. Koorgan had decided bringing back a boar would cheer him up and maybe help Gant not be so upset about the fact that he had traveled a bit farther afield than he had originally planned. Now, he wasn't so sure that going hunting alone was such a good idea.

The trees grew thick and tall here. Little sunlight broke through the high canopy above them. Tall ferns bordered the muddy path. Genisus nervously shook his head and tried to back up. The sound of a snapping branch had Koorgan turning the stallion to face their unseen companion. Genisus released a loud neigh and rose up a little on his hind legs.

"What is it, boy?" Koorgan quietly murmured, his hand moving toward the crossbow attached to the side of his saddle. He had just grasped the weapon when a loud crashing sound came from behind him along with a savage snarl.

Genisus jumped and kicked out as a thickly muscled creature with long, razor-sharp tusks charged from the ferns. The stallion's massive shod hooves connected with the Razor boar's head.

Koorgan loudly swore when he saw four more following behind the first boar. He swung the crossbow around, fitted an arrow, and fired.

The arrow struck the right shoulder of the boar and bounced off. The boars had thick hides. Unless he could get a direct hit to a vulnerable place, the arrows would only enrage them further.

Genisus bucked as two more came at them from the front. Koorgan kicked his heels into the stallion's side, dropping the reins as he fought to fit another arrow.

Genisus vaulted over the boars blocking their path. Koorgan twisted in the saddle and took aim. Behind him, he could see the boar that Genisus had struck lying dead, his skull crushed from the powerful kick he had received. Unfortunately, that still left six more boars.

Koorgan fired a shot and watched his arrow strike true, piercing the boar's skull between its eyes. He didn't wait to watch it stumble and fall. He turned to load another arrow, then ducked, his eyes wide as Genisus passed under a low hanging branch.

In his haste to keep his seat, he bent forward, and the crossbow caught on a low hanging dead branch. The crossbow was ripped from his hands. Koorgan bowed his head to look under his arm, and saw the weapon swinging back and forth. There would be no retrieving it. One of the boars attacked the weapon, snapping the wooden crossbow stock with its massive jaws.

Turning his attention back to the path ahead, he pulled his sword from its scabbard, and slashed backwards when a boar leaped up to grab his arm. The blade caught the beast between his two front legs and split open its chest.

Genisus swerved when another boar came up on his right side, and rammed the boar, crushing it against the trunk of a tree. Koorgan heard the satisfying crunch of bones.

The path ahead of them curved to the left. On the right side was an incline of boulders. Koorgan gripped his sword and leaned in as Genisus started to round the sharp curve.

A vicious snarl split the air as they drew even with the rocks and Koorgan jerked around, bringing his sword up as the beast leaped at him.

Genisus whinnied loudly, stumbled, then kicked out at one of the Razor boars behind them who was trying to bite his hind leg. The combination threw Koorgan off balance.

His sword drove deep into the chest of the Razor boar, but the weight and momentum of the beast knocked him out of the saddle. He landed on his back in the ferns, his long sword still impaling the Razor boar.

Genisus had disappeared along the path with one of the Razor boars still chasing him. Koorgan rolled to his feet, and tugged on his sword, but it was firmly embedded in the boar's spine. He placed his foot on the body to get better leverage, and heard a branch snapping not more than a couple of yards from him.

Twisting around, he found himself face to face with the largest of the Razor boars. His eyes locked on the beady red eyes of the boar as it pawed the ground and rocked its head from side to side. Koorgan's fingers tightened on the handle of his sword, his foot braced on the body of the smaller boar as he slowly removed his weapon from its spine.

The boar emitted a high-pitched screech as it charged him. Koorgan jumped to the side, swinging his sword at the same time. The well-honed tip of his sword connected with the end of the boar's tusk, lopping it off.

Koorgan swiveled when the beast turned in a rage and attacked once more. He swung his sword again, but didn't have enough room between himself and the beast to land a solid blow. The boar slammed into his legs and knocked him backwards. His heel caught on a dead tree half buried in the ferns and he fell backwards.

The sword flew out of his hand and landed in the base of a tree. He turned his head to follow the trajectory, then flipped over the log he had tripped on and lifted it to intercept the charging boar. The beast was now between his position and his only weapon.

He threw the log at the boar and took off at a run, darting between the narrow trunks of two trees as the boar noisily crashed after him. He glanced over his shoulder, then released a loud curse when the ground suddenly collapsed under his feet and he felt himself go weightless for a moment before he hit the bottom of a deep pit.

He fell backward, staring up at the glimpses of blue sky through the distant canopy of trees. The Razor boar's head appeared over the edge, and the boar squealed in rage. Koorgan pushed off the ground and stood up. The boar, realizing that there was no way to get to him without joining him in the pit, turned and scraped grass and dirt down into the hole with his back legs.

"Hey! You miserable beast! I'm the one in the hole, not you," Koorgan growled to the animal.

Koorgan listened as the boar grunted and slowly moved away. Examining the pit he'd fallen into, he quickly realized that it wasn't a trap for an animal, but an old well that had been abandoned, probably hundreds of years ago given how well it had been hidden by fallen trees and debris. Eventually, enough soil had collected over it to make it look like the forest floor.

He ran his hands along the smooth bricks that had been carefully placed to seal the sides. He was lucky there was only a small trickle of water in the well, not enough to pool. The floor beneath the debris that had fallen in with him, was solid rock. Whoever had dug the well had probably gone as far as the rock layer before realizing that the well would never produce.

Koorgan slid his hand along the wall, trying to find a place where he could get a grip. None of the cracks were large enough for his fingers, much less his feet. He looked up at the top of the well. It was at least fifteen feet up.

If he had been anywhere else but on the Isle of the Giants, the distance wouldn't have been much of a problem – well, except for the diameter. While his kind had the ability to grow to enormous sizes, the enchantment did not function on their home Isle unless they were under attack by another race – a safeguard to protect the Isle from their own hot tempers, he suspected.

He spent the next two hours trying to figure a way out. When that failed, he whistled for Genisus. The only response he received was a chorus of imitations by the Coppabirds. Tired, he sank down onto the smooth granite floor of the well, drew up his legs to rest his arms on his knees, and leaned his head back.

"Gant will realize I'm gone and come looking for me," he murmured.

A wry smile curved his lips. He had wanted some time alone and it looked like he was going to get it. It might take Gant days to find him. Koorgan picked up a branch and broke it into little pieces.

His mind swirled with thoughts and he rolled his shoulders to ease some of the tension. Stretching out his legs, he leaned back and relaxed. A small grimace crossed his face when his stomach growled.

"I should have eaten before I left. This will teach me to listen to Gant." Koorgan groaned, and shook his head. "He is so going to enjoy giving me a hard time about this," he muttered with a rueful sigh.

He'd seldom had time alone since becoming the King of the Giants…a long, long time ago. Taking over the responsibilities of the King at such a young age had been unexpected. His parents had been in the prime of their lives before they mysteriously vanished.

Koorgan suspected the Sea Witch was responsible for whatever had happened to them. They had been out negotiating trade deals with the other Kingdoms – and he suspected scouting out a possible future bride for him – and never returned. Their disappearance had coincided with the attack on the Isle of the Dragon. Since that day, he had done the best he could to protect his people as the Sea Witch waged war on the Kingdoms.

Koorgan had sensed the darkness in his kingdom when Magna the Sea Witch had been here. Fearful that it would affect the already hot tempers of the giants, he had restricted all travel and trade with the other Kingdoms to a limited number of merchants.

The Isle of the Giants had been comparatively protected from the Sea Witch's dark magic, and they had become more self-reliant. Out of necessity, they now manufactured or produced nearly all of their products and food, much to the disgust of Ashure. However, their economy was struggling, and they were making do with fewer products they had once taken for granted.

A shudder went through Koorgan. He hated that part of ruling a Kingdom. He could settle the disputes, command their army, but when it came to dealing with trade and economics, he felt like just strangling the idiots who demanded he give more for less. He didn't trust many to do the job either, not after some of the stunts Ashure had pulled.

No one was even an adequate candidate for the appointment, as he had found out after he stubbornly tried to put giant after giant in the position, and they had all been too impatient, impulsive, and too easily manipulated by one emotion or another. Even his parents' closest friend, Agatha, that dainty, wrinkled beauty with her single gorgeous eye and sharp tongue, hadn't been much help. Dealing with the diplomats from the other Kingdoms was just – irritating.

He issued a low grunt of resignation and turned to lie down, raising his arm to use it as a pillow against the hard surface. Staring up at the growing darkness, he sighed and studied the stars through the trees.

He wondered if the alien creature within Magna had been the only one to come to their world. It was hard to imagine something so evil coming from something so beautiful. These were the types of questions he would like to discuss with the woman who would become his wife.

He pondered what it would be like to have a wife like Magika, the Queen of the Isle of Magic. He had met King Oray and Queen Magika on several occasions and been impressed with the Queen's elegance and intellect. She had fought hard to save her husband and stood by her people, even against the horrors and destruction created by Magna and the alien creature.

The kind of wife he wanted… would be someone who he could talk to, even argue with, who wouldn't give in to him all the time. She would be interesting – and independent, but not too independent. The last thing he wanted was a woman who whimpered and whined that she needed his constant attention.

"Like that will ever happen," he muttered in disgust as he thought of all the women he had met so far. "Yes, your majesty. No, your majesty. Whatever you say, your majesty. I swear if I hear that one more time, I'll ban every female from the palace walls. I want a woman who is smart, feisty, and doesn't just lay like a lump of porridge in my bed."

Closing his eyes, a smile curved his lips as he imagined the perfect woman. She would be tall with long black hair that flowed down her back, and full hips that he could grasp in his hands as he…. He released another low grunt, and relaxed, drifting off to sleep, the perfect woman dancing in his dreams.

CHAPTER TWO

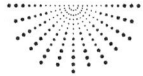

Present Day:

Yachats, Oregon

Ruth opened the door to Mike's house and froze in surprise. A woman was standing on the front porch with her arm raised, about to knock on the door. They stared at each other for a fraction of a second in shock before the woman smiled and held her hand out.

"Hi, are you Ruth Hallbrook?" the woman politely asked.

"Yes," Ruth cautiously answered.

"My name is Tonya Maitland. I'm an investigator reviewing the disappearance of your brother, Detective Mike Hallbrook, as well as the two other women from this area," Tonya explained.

"Finally! Why did you guys take so long to realize that things aren't what they seemed ? You'd think the FBI would be just a little concerned when three people suddenly disappear because they've found some stranger they think they are in love with, never to be heard from again. I mean, even the CIA wanted to know more about Mike's disappearance than the FBI. How messed up is that?" Ruth demanded.

"I… Yes, well, you know how the government can be. I can see that you were about to head out. Do you mind if I ask you a few questions?" Tonya responded.

"No… No, come in. I was just going to go hang more flyers…," Ruth invited, stepping back from the door and waving her hand toward the living room. "Hopefully, you'll be able to answer a few questions, too," she added under her breath.

Tonya gave her a smile and stepped into the house. Ruth walked into the living room and sat down on the sofa. Tonya sat across from her in a matching chair.

"So, what do you know?" Ruth asked.

Tonya gave her an apologetic smile. "Probably nothing more than you do. I was hoping you could share what you know, see if there is anything new to go on. I've just taken over the case and I like to start from scratch," she quickly added.

"New… Yeah, okay. I know that my brother was investigating the disappearance of Carly Tate and Jenny Ackerly, two local women. Not long after that, he disappeared, only to return and give me some outrageously bullshit message about meeting an incredible woman from another world. He said he was going to live with her and told me to have a nice life. He even left me a letter outlining what I should do with all of his stuff. I'll warn you now, you may be dealing with a homicide when I get my hands on my little brother," she snapped before she sank back against the cushions and ran her hand through her shoulder-length hair. "I don't mean that. I just want to find Mike. He's the only family I've got left and we *swore* that we would never forget that. We've always been close – even as kids."

Tonya gave her a sympathetic smile. "I kinda figured that when I drove through town and saw all of the Missing Person flyers," she said.

"Yeah, I think I've decimated a forest or two in the printing of those," Ruth grudgingly admitted.

"Did your brother mention the name of the woman or the country she was from?" Tonya asked.

Ruth shook her head. "No name, and like I said – another world – not a country. That was what was so strange about his message. I didn't get all of the message either. My mailbox was full and didn't record it all," she replied.

"Well, I'm not going to give up looking for your brother – or Carly Tate and Jenny Ackerly. My job is to find out what happened and report it, and I've never failed, Ms. Hallbrook. If you learn anything that you think might help, will you call me?" Tonya requested, pulling a card out of her pocket as she stood.

Ruth nodded, rose to her feet, and took the card. She barely glanced at it before shoving it into her back pocket. She walked to the door, following Tonya. The other woman turned and looked at her with a curious expression.

"How did you know about Cochran embezzling all that money?" Tonya asked.

Ruth released a short chuckle. "I'm a hound dog when it comes to my job. Greed and stupidity are always there in the numbers – if I dig enough, I'll find it, no matter how deep someone tries to bury it under bullshit receipts or illicit Limited Liability Corporations," she answered.

"Good job," Tonya said with a grin. "I'm the same when it comes to finding out what happened to people."

"I really hope you are," Ruth quietly responded.

She watched Tonya descend the steps and hurry to her car. It was strange to see an FBI agent wearing jeans and a plaid button up shirt. Maybe it was a new look to help them fit more readily into their surroundings. A business suit would have stood out like a sore thumb in this tiny rural town.

She lifted her hand when Tonya waved as she pulled away and drove down the driveway. Deciding that standing in the doorway wasn't going to get those flyers hung, she stepped out on the porch, locked the door, and headed for her own car. The remainder of her stack of posters was in the trunk. She'd start at Yachats State Park again before the weather turned crappy. That was where Mike's truck had been found.

"Fingers crossed today will bring some answers," she murmured as she pulled open the driver's door and slid onto the seat.

Several hours later, Ruth pursed her lips and silently issued dire threats to the weather. She had spent the better part of the morning walking the different beach access paths. She'd only retreated when the rain showers became more frequent and the sky grew darker.

Now she hurried through the misty rain over to the information board at the entrance to Yachats State Park. In one hand, she carried several laminated Missing Person notices. In the other hand, she held a professional grade staple gun.

She had graduated from a standard office stapler to a heavy duty staple gun three weeks after she'd found out Mike had disappeared when the jerks here and in town kept removing her posters. She was going to make it as difficult for them to pull out the staples as she could.

Placing a poster against the wooden board, she pulled the lever on the staple gun. The loud pop no longer caused her to wince. Irritation and a major dose of desperation had been two of the emotions that had kept her going over the last several months. Even the hopeful feeling from Tonya's visit this morning had worn off after she replayed their conversation for the hundredth time in her mind.

"If the frigging FBI won't take finding Mike seriously, I'll just have to take matters into my own hands. Mike was a police officer for crying out loud! You would've thought the strange disappearance of one would have made front page news, but *nooooo*! The newspaper relegated the article back to page three below the current fishing report!" she growled under her breath.

Sure, there had been a massive search a little over six months ago, but after a few weeks, it had stopped. All because Mike had called and left an ambiguous message telling her that he was alright.

Stepping back, she gazed at the laminated picture of Mike. Tears of frustration burned her eyes before she blinked them away. She was not the type to let emotion get in her way. No, she was more the type to kick someone's ass.

Okay, most of the time I kick ass with my forensic skill and a calculator, but still, I've brought down some pretty major criminals, she thought as she added another flyer to the board for good measure.

Sure, she might be just an accountant, but she was a damn good one! She could find a missing penny in a dragon's lair and tell you where it was minted. More than one high priced lawyer had paled when she'd walked into a courtroom after an audit, and immediately talked their client into a plea deal.

Turning back around, she headed for her car. She needed to stop by the hardware store for more staples. She would post some new signs in the window while she was there and grab some lunch.

Ruth hurried back to her car, unlocked it, and slipped in. She looked up at the sky and scowled when sunlight broke through. All a person had to do in Oregon was wait and you could get all the four seasons in a matter of minutes. This was why she lived in California – gorgeous weather most of the year if you discounted the earthquakes, fires, drought, and pollution.

She pulled out of the parking lot and waved to the ranger as she exited the park. He would see her again tomorrow – and the day after and the day after that. She had more stones to turn over. There were bound to be a few she had missed the last hundred times she had been here.

Turning on her blinker, she pulled out onto the highway. The beautiful scenery should have been enough to relax her, but all she could think about was returning to Mike's house. She always stayed there when she came, hoping against hope that he would walk through the door.

"How can he just disappear like this? None of his accounts have been touched. The only thing missing from his house are a few personal things – nothing of value! Hell, he didn't even clean out the refrigerator," she said.

There was a certain comfort in mulling over everything out loud. She hoped that by hearing what she was saying, something would click. Ruth was certain there was something she and the authorities were missing.

"When I find the bitch that lured him away, I'm going to rip her hair out one strand at a time until she tells me what she did with him. I'm going to show her what a crazy-ass accountant can do with a letter opener," she growled, her knuckles turning white with anger, fear, and grief.

She sniffed and muttered a curse. Taking a deep, calming breath, she slowed as she entered the town. A short ways down the road, she saw the sign for the local hardware store. Turning on her blinker, she pulled into an empty spot in front of it.

She shifted into park and pressed the ignition button. Reaching over, she grabbed her purse, a handful of flyers, a roll of tape, and the empty box showing her which type of staples she would need. She pushed open the door and slid out.

Out of habit, she locked the door to her car and scanned the area. She'd lived, worked, and traveled to enough places around the world to have a very healthy dose of caution. Hell, if her brother could disappear in a small, picturesque town like Yachats, anything could happen!

She paused as an older couple walked past her before crossing the sidewalk. A faded picture of Mike, the tape coming off of one side, was in the window. She pushed open the door to the hardware store.

Her attention was drawn to a dark-haired young woman standing near the window admiring a small statue of a mermaid. One thing that Ruth had noticed since Mike's disappearance was that she seemed to be more conscious of the smallest details. She had always been good before, but now she was hyper aware.

She set the stack of flyers on top of the paint cans, flashed the woman a brief smile, and leaned over the display in front of the window so she could peel the old tape off of the glass. Ruth could see in her peripheral vision the woman curiously watching her, then coming closer to look at the flyer.

When the woman gasped softly, Ruth immediately turned her head in the woman's direction, her heart pounding. She picked up the flyers and stepped toward the woman whose gaze was locked on the photo of Mike. The woman's eyes jerked up to meet hers and she stumbled back a couple of steps.

"Do you know him? Do you know where he is? Have you seen him?" Ruth demanded as hope flared inside her.

The woman reluctantly nodded, her wide green eyes conveying unexpected depths of grief and guilt. Ruth took another step closer, stopping less than a foot from the woman.

"Where? Where did you see him? When? Please. I need to find him. He is the only family I have left. Please...," Ruth quietly beseeched.

The slight woman glanced in the direction of a burly, handsome man heading towards the counter with a bundle of rope, his attention occupied by the chatty owner of the store, then the dark-haired beauty returned her gaze to Ruth's face, licked her lips, and nodded toward the door.

Ruth gave the woman a brief nod and turned. Pulling open the door, she stepped outside, waited for the woman to exit the store, then followed her when, after looking up and down the street, the slender woman walked toward a narrow alley between the buildings, her long, wavy hair blowing in the breeze. When they'd gone far enough into the alley to have a little more privacy, the woman turned and looked at her.

"Who is he to you?" the woman quietly asked.

Ruth took a deep breath and studied the woman's face as she explained the situation. The lady seemed strange in more ways than one. Her eyes and skin seemed slightly too bright in the gloom of the alley. Her expression was the oddest mixture of impassivity and deep, emotional fragility. "I can't bear to think of him being lost or gone forever. I need to bring him home," Ruth finished, her heart in her throat.

"What if he doesn't want to come home?" the woman hesitantly asked.

Ruth frowned and shook her head. "Why wouldn't he...? You know where he is, don't you?" she suddenly demanded, knowing deep inside that this woman knew exactly where Mike was.

The woman stared at her with haunted eyes. "Yes."

Ruth turned when the woman's attention focused on someone behind her. "Gabe," the diminutive beauty said, her voice strained.

The man's eyes flashed grimly over the flyer in Ruth's hand, his lips tightening for a moment as his gaze clashed with the woman's. The two strangers shared a resigned look before the man's face relaxed. Unease built inside Ruth, and her hand instinctively moved to her purse where she carried a small handgun.

He released a sigh. "How about we get a cup of coffee?" he finally suggested.

She gave a brief, determined nod. "Where?" she asked.

"My place. You can follow us. Kane should be home by the time we get there," Gabe suggested.

Her eyes narrowed with suspicion "How do I know...?" she started to say.

"It will be alright. I... owe your brother a great debt," the woman promised.

CHAPTER THREE

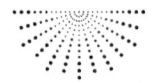

Ruth bit her lip, her eyes moving from the gun she had pulled out of her purse to the truck she was following. She couldn't decide if she was crazy or suicidal. Still, if there was even the remotest chance of finding her brother, she'd take the risk.

She reached into her back pocket and pulled out the card that Tonya Maitland had given her this morning. Holding it between her fingers, she looked back and forth between the card and the road. Still anxiously biting her lip, she switched the card to her other hand and reached for her phone.

Guilt swamped her when she pressed the numbers on her keypad. God, why did she have to be given an extra measure of a moral compass? She *never* used the phone when she was driving unless it was hands-free. Even then, she hated it because it did distract her when she was driving.

Still, after the weird encounter with the couple, and the fact that she was now following them to who-knew-where and something terrible could happen to her, it was better to risk a phone call than disappear without a trace like Mike and the other two women. At least someone important would know to start looking for her. She didn't care what anyone said – something screwy was definitely going on. She pressed the send button and lifted the phone to her ear, impatiently waiting for the FBI agent to pick up.

"Maitland."

"Hello, Agent Maitland, this is Ruth Hallbrook. You said I should call you if I found out anything else about my brother, Mike Hallbrook," Ruth said, slowing to a stop before she took a left turn onto a winding road that led up the side of a mountain.

She had barely begun to speak when she lost cell service. A growl of frustrated curses filled the interior of the car before she tossed her cell phone onto the seat beside her. She had two choices – continue on and hopefully get some answers or chicken out. Since she wasn't willing to lose her only chance at finding out what might have happened to Mike, she kept going.

"I really hope I'm not going to be the next disappearance in Yachats," she muttered under her breath as she pulled up outside a gorgeous house nestled on the base of a mountain.

∽

Ruth tried to keep her expression from showing her curiosity when she pulled up beside the SUV already parked outside the house. A man waiting there immediately went to the passenger side of the truck she'd been following and opened the door for the woman. He helped the woman out before giving her a passionate kiss.

Ruth was surprised because she'd thought the woman was with Gabe, but when she saw the way Gabe took up a protective stance on her other side, she realized the woman was with them both, intimately. She'd read about threesomes before – even an accountant needed a life outside of numbers, especially when she didn't have much of a life otherwise.

She had bombed at handling *one* man. Of course, her ex-husband had been the epitome of a wuss and had been nothing like the two guys currently sandwiching the woman between them! She had given up on trying to find a guy she could tolerate. Most men wilted like a week-old piece of lettuce when they found an intelligent woman with a sharp sense of humor. She didn't purposely try to intimidate them, it just came naturally.

She muttered a soft curse when she opened the door to get out, only to realize that she hadn't unbuckled her seatbelt. She did so, then remembered at the last second to reach over onto the passenger seat and grab her purse. She hastily shoved her small pistol and phone into it before she exited her car.

Ruth warily watched the man called Gabe walk toward her. Out of the two, he was the one who made her most leery of being here alone. There was an air of barely restrained energy about him. She wondered if it was just her presence or if he was always like this.

"I'll tell you this now, I won't let you hurt Magna. She has been through hell and back," he warned in a soft voice

Ruth blinked in surprise. Well, at least she now had a name for the woman – Magna. It was unusual, kind of exotic. It suited the woman.

"All I want to do is find my brother. If she helps me do that, I'll have my lips superglued before I hurt her," Ruth grimly promised.

"That damn stuff works really well," Gabe responded with a surprising chuckle.

"I'd much rather use glue than get stitches any day," she said with a half-smile.

The blond man groaned and shook his head in disgust.

"Oh God! You mean there are two of you in the world?" the man muttered. He shot Gabe a dark scowl before he turned his gaze to her.

"He's a doctor," Gabe mumbled.

"That figures," Ruth responded, relaxing more at Gabe's unexpected sense of humor. There was something about the three, the way they were speaking and acting, that was dissolving her feelings of misgiving. None of them were acting in the least bit threatening. In fact, they fit together in a surprisingly natural way.

"Please come in. Oh, I have to warn you that we have two—" Magna invited.

Ruth grinned when two large Huskies charged her. Laughter bubbled out when Gabe started scolding them. She held her hand out for them to sniff and was immediately rewarded with excited licks.

"Damn it, Wilson! Will you get out of the way? Buck, you'd better not be learning any bad habits," Gabe growled.

Ruth looked at Gabe with an amused expression. "Ah, the sweet sound of pet ownership. I gave Mike a golden retriever for his birthday several months ago," she said before she grew somber at the reminder of her missing brother.

"Wilson is still young," Magna explained with a laugh.

She turned her attention to the man Gabe said was a doctor. He looked vaguely familiar, as if she had seen him around town. He shot her a cautious but friendly smile.

"My name is Kane Field. Would you care for something to drink, Miss…?"

"Ruth Hallbrook," she introduced.

"We have coffee, tea, juice, and beer," Kane offered.

Clutching her purse against her side, she stepped into the kitchen and turned. "Coffee would be great," she replied, looking across to the living room area and the wide expanse of glass doors. "You have a beautiful home."

"Thank you. Please, come into the living room. I love being able to see the ocean from it," Magna encouraged.

Gabe held his hand out and Ruth realized he wanted to take her coat. She shrugged it off, keeping her handbag. Glancing around the immaculate kitchen that would be a chef's dream, she followed Magna into the other room. The entire house screamed peace and unity.

She walked over to the large glass doors and stared out over the treetops at the ocean. She turned when Kane placed a tray on the coffee table. He poured coffee from the carafe into four cups.

"Where is my brother?" she asked.

She sank into the chair across from the couch where Magna and the two men were sitting and picked up her coffee cup, her eyes boring into Magna's. Magna's demeanor was calm, but her eyes spoke of a deep sadness.

"He is in my world," Magna replied.

"Your…. Where is that?" Ruth asked suspiciously. *More talk of 'worlds'. Of course.*

"Perhaps I should start at the beginning," Magna said, opening her hand. In the center of her palm was a necklace with a beautiful green shell. "Take the necklace and turn over the shell. I will be there with you," Magna quietly stated.

Ruth leaned forward, placed her coffee cup back on the tray, and took the necklace from Magna. She looked skeptically at Magna before giving a slight shrug. She turned the shell necklace over in her hand.

Her breath caught in her throat when she found herself on a beach under a starlit sky. She turned in a slow circle before looking down at her feet. She moved her foot, digging the toe of her shoe into the sand. Ruth looked up and stared in wonder at the thick palms and rocky coast of a beach that was far away from the chilly waters of the northern Pacific.

Her attention was drawn to the lone figure of Magna, standing on the edge of the water, staring out at the ocean. Ruth pinched herself to make sure she wasn't unconscious. The twinge of pain convinced her that she was indeed awake.

There were no drugs in the coffee either unless Kane planned to dope us all, she thought before she remembered that she hadn't even taken a sip of her coffee yet, so it wouldn't have made a difference if he had tried to drug her.

Ruth walked across the sandy beach to the edge of the water. She stopped when Magna turned toward her. The intense sadness on Magna's face pulled at her heartstrings. This was a woman who had been touched by great tragedy. Magna turned to look back out at the cove, and Ruth did too, coming closer when she saw a young man in the waves and…creatures. They looked like aquatic dragons, each about as big as a pony, and oh so beautiful. Magical, really.

"That is my cousin, Orion, with the sea dragons." She swallowed, and continued. "My name is Magna. I am the Sea Witch," she intoned as if this were something she had said many times before and she expected it to cause a great deal of fear or awe. When she spoke again, her speech patterns were more normal. "My mother is from the Isle of Magic, one of seven kingdoms in the realm of the Seven Kingdoms. My father is from the Isle of the Sea Serpent. He is what you would call a merman. My home was both above and below the water," Magna explained in a voice laced with grief.

Ruth looked around her once more before her attention fixed on Orion. "We… Are you saying we aren't on Earth anymore?"

"Our bodies are still in the living room of Gabe's house, but our minds are in one of my memories of the Isle of the Sea Serpent. I stored this memory before my body was inhabited by an alien creature that threatened to destroy my world," Magna quietly explained.

Ruth raised an eyebrow. She was about to ask how such a thing was possible when Magna raised her hand and the scene around them faded – as if time was suddenly fast forwarded. Orion and the sea dragons faded away and Ruth heard the sound of laughter.

She blinked in shock when a much younger version of Magna ran down the beach toward them with Orion running behind her. Both of them were laughing.

A flash of light streaked across the sky, drawing Ruth's attention to the object falling to the ocean's surface. The object hit the water with a tremendous splash. The water boiled and glowed before it went dark again.

Magna's anguished voice narrated what was happening. "A creature was within that meteor. It took over my body, most of my mind, and my magic. It forced me to do horrible things to my people. I fought him as best I could, but I knew I would need help if I were to destroy him."

"What did you do?" Ruth asked, feeling frustrated that she was surrounded by so much she didn't understand, like how this shared vision was possible, and frustrated to witness something obviously very bad that seemed so real, but had already happened. She was unable to change anything about it.

"I was finally able to create a spell to destroy it, but in order for it to work, I needed a weapon not of our world that could weaken me. I tried for over a century to end my life, but each time, the creature prevented it. He had learned from my memories how to defend himself against all the weapons of our world," Magna replied.

Understanding dawned when Magna paused. "That is why you needed Mike," she said.

Magna turned and gave her a sad nod. "I was growing too weak to bind the creature to me for much longer. He was hungry for power and would have moved on to a different host, perhaps one even more powerful than I. Over time, I set in motion a series of events. I needed Drago, the Dragon King, to wake. Only his fire, fueled by the heat of vengeance and grief, could burn through the tentacles of the alien. I also needed the power of my cousin's trident to create an electrical field that would stop the alien from communicating with the nightmarish creatures it had created. And finally... I needed the weapon your brother carried, the one that fired the metal ball, to strike me so that the alien would think I was dying," Magna said.

Ruth watched as Magna reached up and touched her left shoulder. Her lips parted in a hiss of surprise. Shot – the metal ball was a bullet.

"Are you telling me that my brother shot you?" she demanded.

Magna smiled at her outrage. "Yes. It was the only way. The creature would have forced me to kill King Oray. With Drago and Orion attacking the alien in the throne room, and the other rulers and their armies attacking its evil forces from the outside, the alien no longer saw me as the most serious threat. I told your brother to save King Oray and escape with the others while I released a spell strong enough to destroy the evil creature. Anyone remaining in the room would have been killed," she explained.

Ruth rubbed her brow. She felt real, but that was about the only thing in this crazy story – fantasy world setting – that did. The more Magna talked, the more it felt like this was dream. Maybe there had been something in the steam of the 'coffee'. Ruth looked back out at the cove. This story wasn't coming from her own mind, that much was certain. So she would keep asking questions and follow this to end.

"But…" She paused, gathering her thoughts to phrase this carefully. Whether this woman was a nutjob with hallucinogens or a bona fide witch didn't really matter at the moment. Ruth's instincts were screaming to be cautious either way. "If the others escaped and you didn't," she continued, "shouldn't you have been killed along with the creature?" Ruth asked, shaking her head in confusion.

"I expected to die…. I wanted to die. My death…. Instead, I woke here," she softly replied with a wave of her hand.

Ruth blinked in shock when the scene in front of her faded and she found herself back in Gabe's living room. She wasn't sure how long she and Magna had been lost in Magna's 'memories', but it had been an incredible tale… and it had the same kind of crazy that was in Mike's message. She wasn't yet sure what she believed – it was a lot to process – but the similarities weren't a coincidence, that much she knew.

She raised a trembling hand to brush back her shoulder-length, reddish-brown hair, and raised troubled eyes to Magna. Say for one, insane second, she did take every bit of this at face value, she'd have to ask herself... If the creature was dead, why had it been necessary for Mike to go back to this strange, alien world?

"But what about my brother? I know he came back to Yachats. He left me a partial message. The damn voicemail cut off too soon," she growled.

"He is in my world. He was with a young witch from the Isle of Magic. She had a family. I suspect he chose to return to the Seven Kingdoms because she could not come here," Magna replied.

Ruth silently rose to her feet and walked over to the row of glass windows. She contemplated her options. Either what she had just experienced was one hell of a hallucination or it was real. As much as she'd like to believe it was all make-believe, there was a part of her that was also hoping that it was real. Another world – hidden away – and Mike was there.

"How do I get to this 'Seven Kingdoms' place?" Ruth asked, turning and looking at Magna with a fierce, determined expression.

Magna rose to her feet and stepped around the coffee table. Ruth swallowed when the young woman stopped in front of her and looked into her eyes with a serious expression. She returned Magna's intense gaze with one of her own.

"Open your hand," Magna requested.

Ruth lifted her hand, and Magna waved her hand over hers. A barely audible hiss slipped from her lips when a red shell, the size of a tangerine, suddenly appeared in the center of her palm. Her fingers wrapped around it.

Magna laid her hand gently over hers. "When you are ready to leave, go to the beach where your brother disappeared, make a wish, and repeat the words the shell tells you. The shell will guide you. Keep the shell close to you. If you ever wish to return here, you will need it," Magna warned.

"I... I can't tell you how strange this all sounds, but if it means finding my brother.... Thank you," she said.

"I hope you find what you are looking for," Magna murmured.

Ruth bent and picked up her purse from its place next to the chair. "We'll see about that. I swear I'm going to wring his neck for giving me a scare," she vowed, straightening with a rueful smile.

She gasped when she saw that Magna's appearance had changed. The woman's hair was still a rich, thick black, but now there were hints of green in it. Her creamy white skin now held a glitter of green that looked suspiciously like scales.

"I'll see you out. The sooner you leave, the sooner you can wring his neck," Gabe suddenly said.

Gabe stepped around and put a gentle but firm hand against her lower back. She started forward when he applied pressure. Still preoccupied by Magna, she nodded, and walked across the living room, through the kitchen to the door that Kane had opened ahead of them. She ignored Gabe's scowl of disapproval when she paused at the door and turned to face Magna one last time.

"Thank you again," she murmured.

Magna bowed her head. "I know what it is like to lose family. I hope you find him," she quietly replied.

"I will. I can be very persistent when I want something," Ruth said with a confident smile.

"Good. Let's go." Gabe stated in a firm tone.

Ruth raised an eyebrow at him. "Geez, where'd she find you? In a cave?" she remarked as he practically pushed her out of the door.

"Close enough," Gabe replied. He didn't say anything else until they were standing next to her car. "Don't say a word about Magna, understand? She's been through enough without someone saying shit about her."

She studied his expression. He truly loved Magna. Her heart softened.

Whether or not Magna was as mad as a hatter, everyone deserved love. Ruth was glad Magna had found it.

"I just want to find my brother. Your secrets, and Magna's, are safe. I don't give a rat's ass where she came from and what she's done as long as she doesn't intend to hurt anyone," she replied, unlocking her car door and opening it.

"She doesn't," Gabe reassured her in a rough tone.

Ruth nodded and slid into the driver's seat. Gabe held the car door, waiting for her to respond. She looked up at him and released a long sigh.

"Then my lips are sealed. Go back to your cave. I'm going to go find my brother," she stated, pulling the door free of his grip and shutting it.

She started her car and shifted it into reverse as Gabe took a step back. In the doorway, she could see Magna and Kane silhouetted by the light behind them. She turned and headed back down the mountain.

Once she reached an area where she had cell phone reception again, she pulled to the side of the road and brought out her cell phone. She stared at the display for a moment before she opened her other hand. She was still holding the red shell Magna had given her. Fingering the delicate lines on it, she swallowed, put her phone down onto the seat beside her, and pulled back onto the road.

"Tomorrow I'll decide who to talk to and how much to say… once I've had a chance to process everything that has happened," she murmured, still gripping the shell.

CHAPTER FOUR

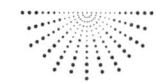

Ruth woke the next morning feeling energized. She had dreamed wild dreams that she could still remember, which was both surprising and unusual since most of the time she did neither. She was also surprised that she wasn't exhausted from her restless night.

She slid out of bed, showered, and dressed in a pair of soft blue jeans and layered shirts. Humming under her breath, she walked into the kitchen. She switched on the coffee pot just as her cell phone barked out a ringtone for 'Who Let the Dogs Out'. She grimaced when she saw the name on the caller ID.

"Agent Maitland," she greeted, making a face at her reflection in the kitchen window.

"Hi, I was hoping you'd call me back last night. I was worried when you didn't," Tonya answered.

Ruth fingered the empty coffee cup and shot a hopeful look at the coffee maker. It was still dripping. She impatiently tapped her finger on the rim of her cup.

"Yes… well, it turned out to be a dud. Nothing new, just the same old, same old," Ruth lied.

"Who did you talk to? Maybe I could follow up and they might remember something more," Tonya inquired.

Ruth made another face. She really wasn't the greatest liar. Mike always said she'd make the worst criminal in history because she was too used to just laying the truth out in the open or shoving it down someone's throat.

"I don't remember their names. Just a couple of locals. Listen, I've just woken up and haven't had any coffee yet. I'm going to grab some. If I remember who they are, I'll call you back. Have a great day," she said, cutting off Tonya's protest before she started.

"Well, that sucked big time. You really need to learn to lie better, Ruth. It would sound better than 'I need coffee'," she muttered.

She sighed when she saw the coffee maker was finished. Pouring a cup of the black brew, she sipped it as she walked over to the kitchen table. She pulled out a chair and reached for the red shell lying on the placemat next to her purse.

Stroking her finger along the smooth surface, it sank in that everything that happened last night hadn't been a dream. Magna, the beach, the thing that had fallen from the sky… she had started seeing the fantasy world before Magna had started talking. She couldn't have hallucinated the story before Magna started telling her about it… and if she hadn't been hallucinating… then all of it was true.

Ruth looked out the window, wondering if she was losing her grip on reality, or if reality was just more than she had ever imagined could be true. That wasn't so strange, was it? Scientists discovered new natural phenomena all the time.

From here, Ruth could see the sand dunes and a glimpse of the water, and in that moment she began to fully let herself believe that another world was out there and Mike was in it.

"I can't believe what happened last night," she muttered to herself with a shake of her head, but she did believe it… she really did.

Lifting the shell, she pressed it to her ear. She didn't hear anything.

Lowering it back to the table, she remembered that Magna had said she needed to go to the beach where Mike went missing. If only she knew exactly which beach that was.

Her hand wrapped around her cell phone. She was about to call Agent Maitland back when she remembered the FBI agent didn't know anything about the case because she liked to start 'fresh'. Ruth started to set the phone back down when a smile curved her lips. There was one other person who might know exactly where Mike had been last – the CIA agent.

She scrolled through her contacts until she found Asahi Tanaka. Taking a deep breath, she pressed the connect button. He answered on the first ring.

"Agent Tanaka," he greeted.

"This is Ruth Hallbrook. I need to ask you a few questions," she stated.

There was a brief silence before he responded. "Normally the questioning goes the other way, Ms. Hallbrook," he replied.

"Yeah, well, I don't think a case like my brother's would normally be handled by the CIA, do you?" she retorted.

Again, another pause. "What questions do you have?" Asahi quietly asked.

"Where do they think my brother's last location was before he went missing?" she inquired.

"Yachats State Park," he responded.

"Yes, but where exactly in the Park? I need to know a more specific location," she pressed, rising to her feet to pace the kitchen floor.

"Does the exact location matter?" he asked.

She paused in mid-turn, remembering Magna's detailed instructions.

"Yes – it matters," she finally replied.

"What have you discovered, Ms. Hallbrook?" Asahi suddenly

demanded.

She dryly chuckled. "What do you think I've discovered?" she parried.

"Where your brother is – and how to get to him," he answered.

Ruth knew he could hear her swiftly inhaled breath of surprise. In that instant, she knew without a doubt why the CIA was involved. Asahi knew about this other world.

"You know about what really happened to Mike, don't you? You know exactly where he is," she said in a barely controlled irritated voice.

Ruth could hear the sound of traffic in the background. Her senses had shifted into high gear and were on hyper-alert. She could feel that familiar tingling sensation rushing up her arms the same way it did when she knew she was about to have a breakthrough during a tough audit.

"I do not know the exact location of your brother, Ms. Hallbrook, but yes, I suspect I know what happened to him and I know a few things about the place where he has gone," Asahi said.

"I don't believe this! How long have you known? Why didn't you tell me? What the hell does the CIA know about this – this place?" she demanded.

"It would be better if I discussed this with you in person," he said.

"How fast can you get here?" Ruth replied.

"I'll be there by this evening," he answered.

"You'd better be, because if what I was told is going to happen, you're about to have another missing person on your hands," she told him in a blunt tone.

She listened to his inhaled breath as she stared down at the shell in her hand. Whatever happened, she wanted to know as much information as possible before she ended up on the other side in fantasyland.

"Do not do anything. I will be there this evening," Asahi replied.

Ruth slowly lowered the phone and placed it on the table. She turned the shell over and over in her hand while she blindly stared out of the window. She laughed softly and shook her head.

"I guess if I'm going to go on a trip, I'd better pack a few essentials," she decided.

∼

Tonya Maitland sat on the bed of the small mom and pop motel situated over the bar. Newspapers, reports, and photos littered the bed. It was the only available workspace since the round table set in the corner contained the coffee maker, ice bucket, and a notebook of advertisements and local interests.

The place was worn, slightly smaller than her bedroom and bathroom back home, but it met her two major priorities – it was clean and it was cheap. As a freelance writer for a variety of small presses and online subscriptions, her budget was as close to zero as she could get it. If it wasn't for the fact that she had a few other articles she had been working on and getting paid for, her accommodations could easily have been a tent on the beach.

She knew that Ruth had misinterpreted her introduction, but as long as she didn't *say* that she was an FBI agent, Tonya figured she wasn't breaking any laws. She *was* an investigator – for the media. Her degree was in investigative journalism, and sometimes that meant letting people draw their own conclusions.

She lifted a piece of red licorice to her mouth and bit down on it. Something was going on here. She could feel it in her bones. Ruth had found out something last night, but for some reason she didn't want to admit it.

"So what is it? A serial killer in Yachats State Park that the police are covering up? Did Mike Hallbrook kill the two women, frame Ross Galloway, then commit a murder/suicide with his dog?" she mused before she shook her head.

No, that didn't make sense. The reports that she had obtained from the case said that Mike Hallbrook had confirmed that Carly Tate and Jenny Ackerly were still alive. The report included a picture of them in some exotic place looking very happy and healthy. He had also exonerated Ross from any wrongdoing.

"Something really weird is going on," she muttered.

She ran her hand through her shoulder-length dark brown hair, then picked up the photo of Jenny, Carly, and a couple of kids. There was something in the background, but it was too small to make out exactly what it was. There was also something funny about Jenny. She sighed when no matter what she did, she couldn't clearly see the small details in the photo. It looked like she needed to make a trip to the local pharmacy to get a magnifying glass.

Sliding off her bed, she gathered the paperwork scattered across it and put it back into the Manila envelope. She looked at the picture one more time before she added it to the collection, then grabbed her oversized bag and slipped the large envelope into it.

She glanced around the room to see if she had forgotten anything. Satisfied that she had what she needed, she made a mental list of what she was going to do. First get the magnifying glass so she could look more closely at the photo. Second, find Ruth Hallbrook and shadow her.

She also wanted to find Ross Galloway. The man had literally disappeared from sight the last couple of weeks. Sure, his mom had passed away, but he hadn't struck her as a momma's boy. About the only things she did know was that he had really lousy taste in the friends he hung out with and he hated fishing for a living.

If she didn't find something soon, she was going to have to return home. She was running out of savings and needed the money from her other jobs to pay the rent on her apartment back in Seattle. She had been sure that if she could solve what was going on here, this would be her big break and some of the bigger news organizations would want to interview her.

Tonya grimaced when her stomach rumbled, reminding her that it was almost lunch time and the only thing she'd eaten was a couple of licorice whips. She opened the door to her room, stepped out, and locked the door behind her. Walking down the hall to the stairs, she half wondered if she was crazy for pursuing this, especially after she learned that the CIA agent had left town. Perhaps she should have chucked it all as well. She was still confused about why the CIA would be interested in the case in the first place.

She descended the stairs, and her eyes widened with surprise when she saw Ross sitting at one of the tables in the bar having lunch. Excitement built inside her.

Perhaps my luck is about to change, she thought.

Tonya casually moved to a table in the corner not far from where Ross was sitting. He was facing the entrance. From her seat, she could see his face. He looked tired – and preoccupied.

Maybe he cared more about his mom than I thought, she speculated.

The door to the pub opened. She wouldn't have thought anything about it if she wasn't watching Ross. His expression changed and his body stiffened. He sat up straight, his eyes locked on the couple who entered.

Tonya recognized the man as Dr. Kane Field. There was nothing special about the guy from what she'd discovered. Her attention was drawn to the woman who moved with a natural grace that few people could pull off. It was almost like she glided across the floor. Dr. Field kept a possessive hand on the woman's back as they followed the waitress through the dark interior to the outside patio area.

Tonya looked back at Ross. His attention was still firmly fixed on the couple. She could see Dr. Field say something to the woman who nodded. A moment later, the good doctor threaded his way to the hallway leading to the bathrooms. She raised an eyebrow when Ross quickly rose from his seat and headed for the woman.

Definitely something going on here, she thought as she noticed the intense determination on Ross's face.

A flash of fear flickered on the woman's face. A series of scenarios formed in Tonya's mind. Ross's dad had been an abusive bastard. Could the woman be a former lover of Ross's who had ended up a victim? While it was possible, the few women she had interviewed who had dated Ross previously said he had his issues, but he was a fun, loving partner. Tonya's nose wiggled when she remembered that all of Ross's lady friends had emphasized the loving part with a giggle full of meaning. One woman had even said that Ross was the hottest lover she'd ever had and she highly recommended Tonya give him a go. Ross never turned down an offer from a pretty face.

Man-whore had been her first thought. Still, nothing led her to believe Ross had inherited his father's enjoyment of abuse. Maybe he wanted to try his hand with this woman.

He'd been sitting outside the woman's house, which is how Tonya had learned about Dr. Field and another man named Gabe Lightcloud. The only conclusion she'd come to was that the good doctor was making a house call – that lasted all night. She was definitely ending up with more questions than answers.

She watched as Ross spoke in a hushed, rapid tone. He appeared to be apologizing, and seemed almost afraid. Tonya's initial thought was that he was afraid of Field and Lightcloud finding him talking to the woman, but he never looked over his shoulder to see if Dr. Field was returning.

Tonya's fingers itched to remove the sunglasses the woman was wearing so she could see her eyes. One of her professors in college had said a person's eyes were a window to their soul. If you could look into them, you would see what type of person they really were and what they were thinking and feeling. She watched as the woman picked up one of the shells on the table and hand it to Ross.

"Do you need anything else?" the waitress asked, blocking her view.

Tonya tried to look around the waitress, but the woman moved with her. "No, just the bill," Tonya replied in a curt tone.

"I'll be right back," the young girl said.

"Shit!" she hissed under her breath in surprise when her view was unblocked.

Ross had disappeared. Dr. Field had returned and so had Gabe Lightcloud. Tonya knew without a doubt that the three of them were in an intimate relationship from the way the men were touching her. They both looked upset for a moment before they began to laugh. It was obvious whatever they were saying had to do with Ross because all three looked in the direction he had disappeared.

The woman rose to her feet and shot Lightcloud a reproving look when he started to follow her. Tonya could feel her lips twitch in amusement. So, the woman could not only handle two men, she could really *handle* two men – *i.e.* she wasn't a submissive.

That rules out being in an abusive relationship with Galloway, Tonya decided.

More curious than ever to discover what was going on, Tonya watched the woman head toward the Ladies room. She quickly tossed enough money on the tray the waitress left to cover her bill and the tip, and rose to her feet to follow the woman. Tonya glanced back at the men at the table before she stepped into the hallway. They were talking, but both had their eyes glued on the direction the woman had gone.

She walked down the hallway and pushed opened the door, turning to the sink when the woman entered one of the three stalls. She pretended to be studying her reflection in the mirror. Her mind raced as she tried to think of what to say to start a conversation.

This was always the hardest part, getting people to open up to a stranger. The first thing was to put them at ease. She looked at her reflection with a critical eye. Reaching up, she ran her hand through her hair and reached for the lip balm in her front pocket.

She took in a deep breath when she heard the toilet flush and the door to the stall opened behind her. Pasting a smile onto her lips, she ran a slow, assessing look over the woman's face. The woman had removed her sunglasses and Tonya blinked as she found herself drowning in the woman's unusual green eyes.

She stepped to the side. "Beautiful day out. I'm so excited that it has finally stopped raining," she said, almost wincing when she used the standard trope of the weather as an opener.

"Yes, it is very beautiful," the woman politely answered.

"I'm not from around here. Do you have any suggestions about what I might find interesting? Oh, sorry, I'm Tonya, by the way," she introduced.

"My name is Magna. I'm afraid I don't know much. I've only been here a few weeks," Magna replied.

Tonya leaned back against the corner. Now she was getting somewhere. Still, there was something off about the woman that was causing all of her warning bells to start ringing.

"Oh, where are you from? I'm from New York," Tonya lied.

"Is New York far from here?" Magna inquired with an expression of uncertainty.

"You don't know where New York is?" Tonya blurted out in surprise.

Magna was definitely wary now, and she glanced at the door. "I have to return to my companions," she replied.

Tonya silently groaned, and moved slightly so that she was partially in front of the door. She lifted her hand.

"I didn't catch where you are from," she said, hoping a more direct approach would get the answer to her question.

Magna stepped around her and grasped the handle of the door. Tonya was forced to move when Magna started to open it. She made sure that she remained partially in Magna's personal space. Indecision crossed through Magna's dark green eyes before she finally gave a vague answer.

"My home is far away from this world. I hope you have a wonderful day," Magna murmured before she exited the bathroom.

"It was nice meeting you," Tonya responded in a distracted voice.

Her gaze was focused on Magna's reflection in the mirror. There was a line of dark green tattoos along Magna's throat. She quickly turned as the door started to close and swallowed the shiver of unease that ran through her – there were no marks showing on Magna now.

She knew what she had seen. It hadn't been an illusion or a trick of the light – Magna had markings along her neck that looked like scales. Leaning back against the sink again, Tonya closed her eyes and pictured the designs in her mind. She would do a sketch later.

Pieces of the puzzle from all the information that she had been collecting began to fall like raindrops in her mind. They landed, connecting, until goosebumps formed on her arms. She opened her eyes and reached for her cell phone. Her hands shook as she punched out the letters to her search. If this piece fit, she knew she was onto something huge!

Her lips parted on a hiss and she rubbed her aching brow. Disbelief coursed through her. The disappearances, Mike Hallbrook's weird message before he'd vanished again, the FBI suddenly dropping the case, the CIA taking over, Ross Galloway's weird behavior, and Magna.... Tonya's gaze moved to the door.

"The CIA handles fucking space aliens?" she whispered.

Tonya straightened when two teenage girls entered the bathroom. Grabbing the door, she pulled it open and hurried out to the main room. A swift glance told her that Magna and her two companions had already left. She gripped her oversize bag, trying to decide what to do, and then she remembered Ruth Hallbrook's strange responses to her call this morning.

"She knows something. Now, to find out what it is," Tonya murmured with growing certainty.

CHAPTER FIVE

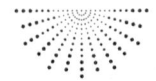

Isle of the Giants:

Koorgan groaned as he stiffly pushed off the ground. The first glimpses of dawn were beginning to break over the forest. He stretched the kink out of his back and rubbed a hand over his hip. There had been an uneven spot on the stone that had made sleeping difficult so he had given up on trying a couple of hours ago. His stomach took that moment to rumble, reminding him – again – that he hadn't eaten since yesterday morning.

He was tired, hungry, and frustrated that Gant hadn't found him yet. He was going to give his friend hell for taking this long, though in all probability, Gant was sitting around a campfire enjoying a nice cup of hot cider just far enough away that Koorgan couldn't tell he was there.

He lifted his fist and struck the stone along the side in frustration. A muttered oath broke from his lips when dirt fell from around the edge onto his head. He nursed his bruised hand against his chest, rubbing it with his other hand to ease the ache.

"Gant! Where in the bloody hell are you? Fine Captain of the Guard you are to leave me stranded in the bottom of this damn pit," Koorgan yelled.

He'd been shouting on and off for the past hour. The only thing he had to show for his efforts was a dry throat and clumps of dirt in his hair. He tried yet again to think of a way out, but with nearly fifteen feet between himself and the top, he was out of ideas.

"Gant! Genisus! Anyone?" he tiredly shouted again, hoping that someone – anyone – would appear.

He leaned back against the wall and looked up. The insane thought flashed through his mind that if no one found him, it was possible that he would actually die here. The thought was depressing. Surely Gant would send the guards out to look for him. The hounds should be able to follow his trail. If nothing else, Genisus would have returned to the palace riderless which should have alerted them immediately that something had happened to him.

"Unless the Razor boar was successful in harming him," Koorgan murmured.

He shook his head. No, the stallion was bred for the hunt. He just needed to be patient. Gant would show up – eventually.

"And he will never, ever let me live this down," Koorgan groaned.

∽

Yachats, Oregon:

The rest of the day seemed to crawl by. Ruth walked the beach, clutching the red shell in her hand. At one point she sat on the rocks and watched an old fishing trawler sail by. She thought she recognized the fisherman at the wheel as Ross Galloway, but the trawler was too far out for her to be sure.

It was getting late by the time she rose and walked down the beach to Mike's house. She was climbing the path through the sand dunes when she saw the headlights of an SUV flash as it turned into Mike's driveway. She stopped at the top.

Through the windshield, Ruth could see Agent Asahi Tanaka behind the wheel. She knew from the area code of his cell number that he had probably not come from nearby. The man must have a private plane at his disposal to get here so quickly.

He exited his vehicle and stood beside it, watching her progress on the path with an intense expression. A wry smile curved her lips when she saw that he was impeccably dressed as usual. She wondered if he knew that his persona screamed government agent.

"Ms. Hallbrook," Asahi greeted with a slight bow of his head.

"You can call me Ruth, Mr. Tanaka," she said, lifting her hand to shake his.

His expression didn't change as he held out his hand. "Ruth," he quietly responded.

"Would you like a cup of coffee or tea?" she asked with a wave of her hand toward the house.

"Tea would be nice," he responded.

"You made good time," she commented as they walked up the footpath to the house.

"The advantage of having connections," he answered.

Ruth wiped her shoes on the mat, unlocked the door, and stepped inside. She kicked off her shoes and placed them in the shoebox next to the door. She chuckled when she saw Tanaka's brief expression of uncertainty.

"You can keep your shoes on if you like. I was on the beach all day," she said with a smile.

"Thank you, but I was taught never to walk in the house with shoes," Asahi replied, quietly shutting the front door behind him and removing his shoes before he followed her to the kitchen.

She filled the electric kettle and turned it on. Opening the cabinet above, she pulled out a canister filled with an assortment of herbal teas and two large mugs.

She filled both mugs with hot water and carried them to the kitchen table. Asahi picked up the canister and placed it on the table. He smiled at her when she raised her eyebrow at the thoughtful gesture.

"My grandfather believed that a man should know his way around the kitchen," he calmly explained.

"Kudos to such a wonderful grandfather," Ruth said.

"He was indeed a wonderful man," Asahi agreed.

Ruth waved to the seat across from her, and sank down onto her own chair. She removed a mint tea bag from the canister, and they each prepared their tea, silent as they completed the simple task.

"Tell me what you know about the Seven Kingdoms," she quietly requested.

Asahi stared at her for a moment before he placed his tea bag on the saucer in the center of the table. Ruth could see his body relax and for a brief moment, she saw a touch of vulnerability in his eyes before he looked down at his cup. She leaned forward and waited.

"It is a world where dragons exist and mermen swim beneath the seas. A world where magic flourishes, pirates roam, and monsters dwell under the rule of an Empress who protects them," he said.

"But… how? How can any of this be real and no one knows about it?" she demanded, wrapping both of her hands around the warm mug.

He looked up at her. "One person knew about it before your brother and these missing women," he replied.

Ruth's eyes narrowed with interest. "Who?" she asked.

Asahi looked out the window at the ocean beyond the dunes. "My grandfather," he replied.

"Your… Are you saying that your grandfather went to this… world? How? Did he come back? Of course he came back otherwise you wouldn't know about it," she muttered with a shake of her head.

"My grandfather's trawler was discovered floating off the coast – empty save for the fish in the hold. For years, my grandmother and father would walk to the rocky point and look out at the sea, begging it to return their Aiko to them. Day after day, year after year, my grandmother went. Soon, my father stopped going with her. One day, she did not return. When my father went to search for her, he found a young man holding her limp body," he explained.

"Did the man kill her?" Ruth asked in horror.

Asahi shook his head. "No. My grandmother had died of a heart attack and fallen in the water. The young man…." He looked at her with a sadness in his eyes that made her chest ache. "The young man was Aiko Tanaka – my grandfather. He had not aged a day from the time he had disappeared."

"How long… how long was he missing?" Ruth breathed, clutching the mug so tightly she was surprised it didn't shatter in her hands.

"My grandfather was gone for forty years. My father could have been his father, instead of the other way around," he said.

Ruth shook her head in disbelief. "How do you deal with something like that? What did your father do? How did the police handle it?" she murmured.

"My grandfather told the truth. He had found her and brought her to shore, but was unable to revive her. A coroner confirmed that my grandmother had died of a heart attack. My father – my father was not as forgiving. I was seven when my grandfather reappeared. My grandfather tried to explain to my father what had happened to him, but my father refused to believe him. He stormed out of the house that night – never to return. A deer was in the road and he swerved to miss it. He went over the cliff. After the funeral, my grandfather took me back to California and raised me," Asahi finished.

"Wait! I mean, okay, things were a bit different back then, but how do you know that this guy really was your grandfather? I mean, things like this don't happen, surely...," Ruth's voice faded when Asahi reached into his jacket pocket and pulled out an envelope.

He slid the envelope across the table to her. "I had the same questions. It is one of the reasons I went into the CIA. I wanted answers. The problem was, the more answers I found, the more questions I had. I had my grandfather's records from the Japanese-American Internment camp. There were photos and fingerprints. They matched perfectly. I also had his personal effects. My grandmother kept them after he disappeared. DNA from the hair sample matched Aiko," he explained.

Ruth pulled out the folded papers of the detailed reports and the DNA results. She read through them before placing them back in the envelope. Next, she picked up the pictures. Her breath caught when she saw a picture of Asahi's grandmother and grandfather when they were young standing side by side, then a picture of Asahi and Aiko standing side by side. There was no doubting that the man was the same – except for the sadness in his eyes.

"Did he tell you what happened to him?" she asked, her throat tight with emotion.

"Yes," he said.

Ruth looked at him. "What are you going to do?"

"I'm going to go with you," he stated in a firm, quiet voice.

~

Tonya sat in her car along the side of the road, and watched Asahi walk out to his rental car.

"I knew it!" she hissed, slapping the steering wheel with the palm of her hand.

She had given up on Ross when she saw him pulling away from the dock in his trawler, but after a quick stop at the pharmacy for a magnifying glass, a couple of bottles of water, a six pack of Hershey Chocolate bars with Almonds, several packs of snack crackers, and a megadose bottle of pain reliever, she had set her sights on finding Ruth. She had been sitting in her car outside Mike Hallbrook's house for hours… watching and waiting.

Two trips to a nearby stand of trees had provided relief for her bladder, but her stomach was wishing that she had grabbed more than junk food. Now, she felt like all the discomfort had been worth the wait.

Asahi Tanaka opened the back door of his rental car and pulled a black duffle bag out of the back seat. The lights flashed, indicating that he had locked the doors to the vehicle.

"It looks like it is going to be one long night," Tonya grumbled.

She groaned and scrunched down in the seat. She grabbed her heavy jacket from the passenger seat when the lights in the house came on. It was already cold and would only get colder as darkness descended.

CHAPTER SIX

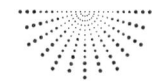

Ruth drove to Yachats State Park late the next afternoon. Asahi followed her in his rental car. She kept glancing up at the mirror to make sure that he was there.

A part of her worried that she'd made a mistake sharing the information Magna had given her with Asahi. What if she'd inadvertently broken the spell that was supposed to take her to Mike? Her eyes moved to the red shell tucked in the cup holder. She had lifted it to her ear a thousand times since Magna had given it to her and still not heard a sound – not even the hum of the ocean.

She had reluctantly allowed Asahi to try it last night. He had not heard anything either. Maybe this was all an elaborate joke. It was still possible that Dr. Field had slipped something into her coffee and she had imagined them corroborating her beach hallucination.

Except you never drank any of the coffee, she reminded herself, *so if it was in the steam, they would have drugged themselves too. That meant it wasn't harmful, but it's very possible we were all loopy that night and I just didn't notice.*

The more she thought about it, the more she wondered if that was what had really happened. It made a hell of a lot more sense than some fantastic magical world where dragons, witches, and monsters lived could really exist.

"But... What about Asahi's grandfather?" she murmured to her reflection in the rearview mirror. Could it be that Asahi was kidnapped as a child by a man who looked like the pictures of his grandfather and later faked the matching DNA? Asahi had recognized the name, though – *The Seven Kingdoms*.

She was a facts type of person. Spell it out, and she could decipher the hell out of it. This was not facts – it was pure, unadulterated fiction to the nth degree. Yet….

I want to believe, and that is where the problem lies. You want it to be real, Ruthie, and you gotta prepare yourself for the possibility that after all this, you'll find out it's not, she thought with a sigh.

Unfortunately, that was something of a pattern with her. She had been this way for the last thirty-three years of her life! One failed marriage later, and she was still making the same mistakes. She just kept searching for a pot of gold at the end of the rainbow – a brother who was alive and happy, a husband who wasn't a pushover, a career that was slightly less frustrating. Since that was about as likely to happen as her being transported to the top of the Beanstalk where the giants lived with their Golden Goose, she might as well suck it up, Buttercup, and accept that fantasies didn't really exist any more than magical Kingdoms.

She shot her reflection a wry grin. "Oh well. I am what I am… so, here we go again," she told herself.

Turning on her blinker, she turned into the entrance to the Yachats State Park, and pulled up to the ranger kiosk. Asahi pulled his car to a stop behind her. The kiosk was empty, of course, with the posted hours informing visitors that the park closed at sunset. She grimaced as her moral compass tapped her on the shoulder again.

"Well, if you are going to break the law, at least you can do it with a CIA agent right behind you," she mused.

She slowly pulled through, wincing when she went over the speed bump. She sped up and headed for the parking lot where Mike had left the Ranger's truck with a note the second time he had disappeared. Apparently, he'd popped up in this State Park and needed to borrow the truck to get back home... and then came right back here to the park. A sense of unease ran through her when she looked at the tall trees casting shadows along the winding road.

"Why couldn't Mike have disappeared in downtown L.A.? I could handle a city. For that matter, why did I listen to Asahi about doing this now? Who cares if people see us magically disappear? We could end up in some supermarket tabloid feature as alien beings, but no, I had to listen to a CIA agent who has probably watched more out-of-this-world movies than I have! 'Let's do this at twilight instead, since that is the witching hour when magic, a portal to another world, a few monsters, and dragons, and God knows what else can suddenly appear!' he says and I just say 'Okay, that sounds great' like I know what he is talking about. How good is it sounding now, Ruthie?" she muttered under her breath as she pulled into the empty parking lot.

She shifted her car into park and sat with it still running as she looked at the path that led to the beach. She jumped when she heard a knock on her window. Asahi was standing next to the driver's door.

"Obviously he doesn't have the same misgivings," she muttered as she turned off the engine and unbuckled her seat belt.

She grabbed her oversized purse and the red shell out of the cup holder before opening the door. She shut the door and locked her car, then leaned back against the side of the vehicle and moodily stared at the path. She silently went through the list of every curse word she could think of as she called herself a fool. It didn't matter, she knew she was still going to try using the shell.

"Are you sure this is where the woman told you to come?" Asahi asked.

Ruth nodded. "She said to go to the beach where Mike disappeared, make a wish, hold the shell to my ear, and say the words that I hear. I know you want to come with me, and I'm not about to turn down having someone there with a little more skill in fighting than I have, but you do understand there is no guarantee this is going to work in the first place, much less work for both of us," she warned.

His expression became grim. "Yes, I am aware. Even so, this is the first true break that I've had in all the years since my grandfather shared the story of his journey," he said.

Ruth nodded, and glanced up at the sky. It would be dark as hell in less than an hour. If they were going to try to find the spot where Mike had disappeared, they would need to get moving.

"Well, I guess we'll see what happens," she said.

Asahi stepped to the side and held his hand out for her to go first. Ruth slid the strap of her large bag over her head and walked across the parking lot to the path. There she paused for a moment, swallowing her reservations before she started up the winding trail that led to the beach.

∼

Tonya turned off the lights to her car and slowly pulled up to the edge of the parking lot, watching as Ruth Hallbrook and Asahi Tanaka talked for a moment. It looked like something serious was going down.

Her gut had been right about Ruth lying after all. She had begun to doubt her instincts. Camping out in her car for over twenty-four hours had sucked. She had been on the verge of giving up when Ruth and Tanaka had suddenly exited the house. They had moved with a sense of purpose – like they were on a mission, and then they drove off in separate cars, Tanaka following Ruth.

When they eventually turned on the road leading to Yachats State Park, Tonya knew something was definitely going down. There was no reason to wait until it was almost dark to go to the park when the day had been relatively clear.

They disappeared up the path leading to the beach, and Tonya pulled into the parking space closest to the entrance. She hurriedly shifted her car into park, grabbed her bag, camera, and jacket, and slid out, closing the door quietly behind her.

Jogging over to the path, she paused and listened for any unusual noise before she silently followed them. Excitement built inside her. This was it – she could feel it.

This is going to be my big break, she thought as she stayed just close enough to catch an occasional glimpse of Tanaka's back up ahead of her.

∽

Ruth decided that she totally needed her head examined as she focused on not falling on her butt along the uneven trail. She also thought of all the ways she could kill Mike. Behind her, she could hear Tanaka's muffled footsteps. Knowing he was there was probably the biggest reason she didn't turn tail and run back to the safety of her car.

She slowed as she stepped out of the thick line of trees that bordered the long, narrow cove where her brother was supposed to have last been. The moon was high in the sky tonight and its light glistened on the rough surf. A strange sense of peace settled over her as she drew in a deep breath of the salty air.

"Oh, Mike, I miss you. I wish I was there with you," she whispered, staring out at the ocean.

"Do you hear anything yet?" Asahi asked from behind her.

Ruth started with surprise, having forgotten for a moment that Asahi was there. She lifted the red shell in front of her and stared down at it before she held it up to her ear. She shook her head and lowered it back to her side.

"Not yet," she said.

"We can walk down the beach," he suggested.

"Yeah, but which way?" she asked, partially turning to look at him.

"Tracks were found heading north. We can try that," he said.

"North, north...." Ruth muttered.

She frowned and looked both ways along the beach as she tried to remember her directions. She was hopeless without a GPS. Asahi pointed to the right.

"That way is north," he said with a hint of amusement in his voice.

"Man invented GPS and compasses so that women did not have to learn how to find North – and so men didn't have to ask for directions," she retorted.

"I did not know that," he replied with a straight face, but his eyes glittered with humor.

She stepped down off the trail onto the beach and started walking north. They walked in silence as the sun set. For a moment, the sky looked like it was lit with fire before beautiful hues of red, pinks, blue, and purple began to color it like a watercolor painting.

"The sky is so beautiful," she murmured.

"Sailors have a saying – red at night is a sailor's delight; red in the morning…," Asahi started to say.

"… Sailors take warning," Ruth finished with a half-smile at his surprised look. "Our mom loved to fish. She was always dragging Dad, Mike, and me out on the water."

"I'm sorry about your loss. I read about your parents' deaths when your brother went missing," he replied.

"It sucked losing them both so close together. I think that is another reason why Mike and I were so determined not to lose touch with each other. We realized how fragile life can be. We thought we'd have more time with our folks. They were both too young to die," she said.

Tanaka nodded. "I understand. Do you hear anything yet?" he asked.

Ruth blinked, surprised that she had forgotten for a moment why they were there. She lifted the shell to her ear. Her breath caught and she suddenly stopped.

"What is it?" Tanaka demanded.

"I hear something. It is very faint, but – but I hear something," she whispered, turning to look at him.

"May I?" he requested, holding out his hand.

Ruth frowned and reluctantly nodded. She handed him the shell and watched as he lifted it to his ear. She waited, holding her breath. After a minute, he held the shell back out to her.

"Well?" she asked.

He shook his head. "Whatever spell has been placed on the shell, it must be for your ears only," he quietly replied.

She lifted the shell to her ear, feeling a sense of urgency coursing through her veins. She turned and began walking again, this time even faster than before. The further she went, the more distinct the unintelligible words became. They sounded – alien.

"What is it?" he asked, easily keeping pace with her.

She briefly glanced at him. "The words are becoming clearer, but they are foreign. I don't know what language they are in," she said.

"Can you repeat them?" he asked.

She shook her head. "Not yet. Some are still too faint," she murmured.

Tanaka nodded. They hurried down the beach. With each step, the words became louder, clearer, and she was able to start memorizing them.

"Stop!" she ordered.

She closed her eyes, listening to the words over and over and over again. Her lips began to move, silently repeating them. There was still one word that she was having trouble wrapping her tongue around.

When Ruth felt ready, she tuned everything out around her and kept her eyes closed as she repeated the words out loud. *"Abi nar aquar ta maylamay t'mu quickta roe-rey-lamay ta magic—"*

For a fraction of a second, her concentration broke when she felt Tanaka's hand on her arm and heard a woman's voice calling out – and she couldn't remember the last word. She ignored everything else and pulled the word out of her memory. *"…Giantshrink."* She cringed. Her tongue had gotten twisted on the word, but she immediately corrected it, " *– Gia-shrek."* She opened her eyes to look at Tanaka.

Her mouth dropped open, her eyes grew wide, and she could feel a scream building in her throat. Instead of Asahi Tanaka standing beside her, she was staring into the drooping eye of a slug twice as big as she was!

Her scream filled the air as she stumbled backwards, fell over a log, and stared up in disbelief at a very, very, *very* strange world.

"I'm not in Yachats anymore," she whispered in horror.

CHAPTER SEVEN

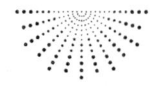

Koorgan slid down against the wall of the well, placed the fist-sized nut that had fallen from the tree above him on the floor, and used a rock to crack the shell.

The meaty interior helped stave off the gnawing hunger in his stomach, but it wasn't exactly a feast. He was about to spend his second night in the bottom of this forsaken pit, and he wasn't sure if he was more furious with his own stupidity for ending up at the bottom of it or at Gant for not finding his miserable hide yet.

In the end, he placed most of the blame on himself and his impulsive decision to go off on the hunt alone. He knew Gant would not stop looking for him until he was found. He just needed to be patient – which wasn't exactly his strongest suit.

On a positive note, he reasoned, he'd definitely had more time to himself, time to think – and dream. Last night he'd dreamed of a strange woman with flashing eyes and lips that made him hard. His subconscious seemed to be surging with fanciful thoughts now that he didn't have anything better to do. He didn't recognize the woman from any of the Kingdoms he had visited before. Even the world around her had been unfamiliar to him.

"It won't matter what I wish for if Gant or someone else doesn't find me," he grumbled as he stretched his legs out and looked up at the sunlight beginning to wane through the canopy above him. "Goddess, if you are listening, I am not too proud to ask for a little help here. Just a dash more would be nice."

With a sigh, he leaned his head back, and wondered what his fate would be as he enjoyed his meager meal.

⁓

"Asahi! Agent Tanaka! Damn it all to hell! Tanaka, where are you?" Ruth shouted. She held a stick in both of her hands as she turned in a tight circle. Her heart fluttered like a hummingbird's wings.

She swiveled when she saw a leaf move. It was the damn slug slithering on his way. Obviously, he wasn't in the mood to listen to her barely controlled hysterics.

Ruth didn't know where in the hell she was, but clearly the spell hadn't worked the way it was supposed to because Mike was not standing in front of her.

Once the slug was gone, she took a moment to take in her surroundings. It was growing darker, which was not helping her temperament or her nerves. Her hands trembled as she braced the stick against her side and fumbled for her cell phone.

It took a few tries, but she shone her light on her surroundings – and wished that she hadn't. Everything was huge! Afraid the light would attract another bug the size of the slug, she turned off the light.

"Shelter…. Remember the stuff Dad and Mike showed you. If you get lost, find shelter. That is the first thing. Stay where you are and find shelter until the search party arrives. Only there won't be a search party because nobody knows where the hell I am – including me!" she muttered, looking around desperately for a safe place to spend the night.

She clutched her cell phone against her chest as she held the stick out and worked her way to a fallen mushroom the size of a large car. She peered under it to make sure no bugs had already taken up residence. Poking the area with the stick in her hand, she finally bent and stepped under the soft underside of the mushroom. She sat down on the ground and pulled her purse into her lap.

"Well, Ruth, you wanted to know if Magna was crazy and now you have your answer. My next big question is where in the hell am I, and how do I get myself out of this mess?" she muttered to herself in a wobbly voice.

She sighed, leaned her head back against the stem of the mushroom, and braced the stick between her jean-clad legs. Wrapping her arms around her purse, she tried to make herself as small as she could. Thankfully, she had chosen to wear her black hoodie jacket. She pulled the hood over her head.

"Please don't let anything eat me. I would really be pissed, and I swear I'll give whatever does heartburn for the rest of its life and haunt Mike forever," she whispered.

Laying her head back, she stayed awake as long as she could, but eventually, she fell into a light, restless sleep, waking frequently when she heard a sound too close for comfort, and falling back asleep when whatever it was passed by her concealing mushroom shelter.

∾

Early the next morning, Ruth irritably slapped a broad leaf the size of a king-size bedspread out of her way. Her morning had gone from bad to worse when she woke up to find that she was not having a nightmare. The world was still huge! She was extremely unprepared for this adventure and she knew it.

"Son-of-a-bitch! I swear I said the words right – the second time. There was like a millisecond before I corrected that last word! This whole freaking place is right out of Gulliver's Travels. Really? Just say the words that the shell tells you to say and it will take you to your brother? Yeah, right! I made one little mistake – that I immediately corrected, may I point out – but does the shell take that into consideration? Hell no! I've slid down a frigging crazy hole to where the dad shrank his kids," she ranted.

She grumbled a long stream of curses as she crawled over yet another huge log. She was tired from the night of fitful sleep, dirty from stomping across miles of forest, and pissed off as hell. The only good news was the sky was beginning to turn light, and now she could see where she was going.

"Why is it my fault that I couldn't understand what the damn spell was saying? Give me the words in English and there wouldn't have been a problem. Hell, give it to me in Italian or Spanish or French or even Japanese or Mandarin Chinese and I could have said it, but no – give me the damn spell in a language that I've never heard before and then get pissy because I misspoke *one… frigging… word*!"

She lifted a hand to her hair and shuddered when she saw a spider the size of a school bus working on a web. So far, she'd seen bugs the size of cars and she'd run into an old spider web that had sent her screaming and running like a banshee trying out for the Olympics. That was no small feat since she was *not* a runner. Sprinting through an airport – yes, she could do that; running a marathon – absolutely hell no.

A shudder ran through Ruth at the memory. She was lucky she had only tangled with a few stray strands of it. Steadying herself, she climbed over another log and under a leaf. Then, tired, she sat down on a stick, and rested her purse on her lap.

She opened it and pulled out her small compact mirror. A grimace of distaste flashed across her face. Pulling out her comb and a travel pack of facial wipes, she cleaned her face and neck, and combed her hair. Replacing the items, she searched for her lip gloss. She found it, and a few items she had forgotten about in the bottom of the purse. A quick swipe had her smacking her lips in relief.

"Okay, what next, Ruth?" she asked herself. "You said the damn words and it obviously took you someplace. The first thing is to find a map or someone, preferably my size, who can lead me to Mike."

She released a tired sigh and looked up at the soft, early morning sky. What would be perfect would be to find *Mike* so she could get them the hell out of this nightmare – she just needed to figure out how to do that. Maybe his witchy girlfriend could do her magic like she did before and send them home. That would be a hell of a lot easier.

Ruth glumly scanned the forest. It felt like she had traveled ten miles, but in reality – at her size – she had probably only covered a few yards. She bit her lip and looked down at the tips of her boots. They were covered in dirt. She could feel a full blown pity party coming on – and then she heard a strange sound.

Tilting her head, she listened. Her eyes widened in delight and she stood up when she heard someone cursing vehemently. It sounded as if someone else was having just as good a day as she was.

Ruth pushed aside the leaf and ducked under the stem of a plant. She hurried as fast as she could in the direction of the guy's voice. She was getting closer.

Pushing a leaf out of her path, Ruth gasped when she almost fell into a humongous hole in the ground. Her arms pin-wheeled and she stumbled backwards, almost losing her footing.

Shaken, she carefully inched forward and looked over the edge of the pit. Her mouth dropped open and she gaped at the size of the man trying to climb the slick wall. Her heart sank, and she stared down at the top of his head in disbelief.

Holy hell! The guy is a freakin' giant! she thought in stunned horror.

CHAPTER EIGHT

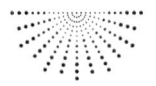

"No, I am not going to help him.... Yes, you are, Ruth Eleanor Hallbrook! You can't leave the poor guy down there!" Ruth argued with herself, pacing back and forth.

Why not? her bad side reasoned. *He's as big as a skyscraper. Surely, he'll figure out a way to climb out of there!*

Even as big as he is, the hole is too deep and the sides are too smooth! her good side countered. *He could die, and then how would you feel?*

She stopped her pacing and growled. She ran her hands through her hair in aggravation. She was so tired of this overdeveloped sense of a civic duty! Why couldn't she just be like the other half of the world who didn't give a damn?

"Because you are a product of your overachieving, good Samaritan upbringing. Argh! I really hate my good side sometimes," she growled in self-disgust.

Then she turned her mind to figuring out *how* she was going to help him. She was the size of a six-inch ruler – with her boots on! How in the hell was she supposed to help King Kong get out of the mess he was in? She paused and closed her eyes. Perhaps that wasn't the best analogy to use.

"At least the heroine lives in the end, even if the poor ape becomes roadkill," she muttered.

Opening her eyes, she turned around and walked back to the edge of the hole. She placed her hands on her hips and took another critical look at the Jolly Green Giant's situation.

"So what am I supposed to do? Toss him down a stick? That's really going to help!" she retorted.

Cursing under her breath, she looked around. The guy needed a rope big enough to hold him, and she could barely climb over a twig!

Blowing her bangs out of her eyes, she stomped along the rim of the hole. She stopped when she came to a long stick the size of a tree back home. Bending, she tried to pick up the end of the stick. It felt like it weighed a ton! She sighed. It wouldn't have helped him anyway.

Ruth rubbed her hands along the sides of her jeans, and kept looking around. Her eyes lit on a small pebble. It wasn't much larger than a watermelon to her. She bent and lifted it into her arms.

Ugh, feels like I'm carrying a boulder! she thought, but she needed to get the giant's attention somehow. She stumbled back over to the edge of the pit. The guy was right below her, trying to climb up the wall again. She pursed her lips and grunted under the weight of the pebble as she lifted it as high as she could before propelling it forward with all her strength and releasing it. The pebble barely cleared the side before it bounced off the smooth wall on its way down.

The giant didn't even look up.

"Argh! I always did suck at sports," she groaned.

She ran her hands through her hair and glanced around again. She could see absolutely nothing that would help. Everything was too damn big or heavy for her to lift. Biting her lip, she began pacing again. She needed to use her brain better, not her limited brawn.

"Okay, think Ruth. You're on a deserted island and a plane flies over. How would you signal it?" she queried. She stopped as an idea hit her. "Yes!"

She hurried over to the large pebble where she had left her purse. Picking up her bag, she opened it and rummaged around the inside until she found the small compact mirror that she had used earlier. She paused when she found the dog whistle that she had picked up for Mike to try with Charlie. She doubted that it would be of much good, but who knew, maybe giants could hear at the same frequency as a dog.

Deciding she would try the whistle first as it was the easiest, she put it to her lips and blew three long blasts of air. She paused for a moment, listening, before doing it once more.

Nothing.

With a sigh, she dropped the whistle back into her purse.

Okay, Plan B, she thought.

She gripped the small compact mirror and searched for an area where the sun was peeking through the trees. There was a large spot about halfway around the hole.

She made her way around the hole, feeling like she had just covered the length of a football field by the time she reached the spot. She would have had a very long list of colorful words if the spot had moved more than an inch or the sun had gone behind a cloud, but it was just as bright when she finally arrived.

Standing in the sunlight, she opened the compact mirror and aimed it so that the sun reflected off of it. It took a couple of tries, but she was able to direct it in front of the guy who was really cursing up a storm by now.

"What the…?" the man said, looking at the dancing light.

She giggled when he reached for it. This was like playing with Charlie and the laser light. Feeling very pleased with herself, she moved the light and grinned when he reached for it again.

Ruth figured she might as well have a little fun just in case this was her last hoopla. She was trying really hard not to think of what the giant tried to do to Jack in the fable. Of course, Jack had just completed a home burglary and stolen the giant's prized possession. She would have tried to stomp on the little turd, too, if he'd broken into her house.

"Hey, you! Big guy! Up here," Ruth called down, flickering the light up the wall.

"Woman, I need assistance. Toss me down a rope or a vine," the man called up.

Ruth resisted the urge to roll her eyes. *The guy has no idea. His face is going to be priceless when he gets a look at me – unless this is normal. Worst case scenario, I leave his ass there and run like hell. Self-preservation is healthy and natural and it trumps altruism,* she thought with a wry grin.

Ruth leaned as far as she could over the side without falling into the hole. "Yeah, well, there's a little bit of an issue with that. The only thing I can throw is a twig and that's not going to do you much good unless you want to pick something out of your teeth... preferably not my bones, of course," she added under her breath. "I'm like out of ideas here. Do you have any? Because I have to tell you, I'm totally out of my element at the moment!"

∽

Koorgan turned toward the voice of the woman. His eyes swept over the rim of the hole. He was about to express his frustration to the unhelpful female when he finally caught sight of her standing at the edge of the well. She was staring down at him with her tiny hands on her tiny hips.

His eyes widened and his mouth dropped open for a moment when he saw that she hadn't been lying to him when she said she couldn't throw him a rope or a vine. He frowned as he stared at her. He had never seen anyone like her before – except, well, in his dreams.

"Who are you?" he demanded, stepping back against the wall so he could see her better without the sun shining in his eyes. "*What* are you?"

"My name is Ruth Hallbrook, I'm human, and don't ask me what happened. There is some seriously weird shit going on that I don't have a clue how to fix yet. So, let's focus on you. Do you mind me asking how on earth you ended up down there?" she asked.

Koorgan raised his eyebrow and grunted. "I fell in while I was hunting. The ground gave out under me," he answered.

She snorted; disgust clearly evident in her expressive face. For someone so small, she had a lot of attitude.

"It serves you right for hunting a poor, defenseless animal. Maybe the next time you decide to go hunting, you'll think twice about it," she retorted.

"A Razor boar is hardly defenseless," Koorgan replied dryly. "What are you doing here?"

She glanced around with a frown. "Rescuing you if I can find a way to do it, and looking for my brother, Mike. A woman named Magna gave me a shell that was supposed to take me to him if I made a wish and repeated the words I heard in it. That is fine and dandy if you can understand the damn language. I screwed up on the last word. It's amazing how much one word can change things. By the way, what's your name?"

Koorgan slowly rotated as she walked around the edge of the hole. "I am Koorgan, King of the Giants, my Lady," he replied with an amused grin.

She paused and looked down at him with a skeptical look before shrugging. "Well, your Highness, you aren't too high and mighty at the moment," she observed with a grin of her own.

"I am well aware of my current predicament, my Lady. As you will be of no help, perhaps you can disappear to wherever you came from and leave me to my humiliation," he growled.

She stopped and looked down at him. "Oh, ye of little faith. Just keep your britches zipped, Koorgan, King of the Giants. We'll figure something out," Ruth replied with a wave of her hand.

"Keep my…. What a strange creature," he muttered with a shake of his head.

He had never heard speech like this before. What type of words were zipped and britches? He had no idea what she meant. Pacing back and forth in the narrow area, he spent the next hour thinking about the strange little female and wondering how the hell he was going to get out of the hole he was stuck in.

Gant obviously needs to train his search hounds better. I don't think it has ever taken him this long to find me, he ruefully thought.

He kept glancing up at the top of the hole for any sign of the woman. Perhaps he was delusional. How could there be a miniature human? He knew Mike Hallbrook – or at least had met the human. He was a normal size person, unlike Ruth.

The longer she remained gone, the more he worried that something might have happened to the woman. What if an insect or other creature had attacked her? She would be defenseless!

He had no idea where the woman had disappeared to. The only sounds were the occasional song of a bird. He paused when he heard the sharp snap of a stick breaking. It sounded loud and close.

"Gant! Is that you? Damn it, man. I need to get out of here. There is a woman…," Koorgan shouted.

No one answered him. Another half an hour passed, and then his eyes widened in surprise when he saw a few small pieces of fruit twisted into the threads of a sticky spider web. They were dangling from the tip of a long, thin stick. Then he saw Genisus's mouth chomp on one of the fruits. The horse neighed in satisfaction.

"Genisus! How...?" Koorgan exclaimed in shock.

Ruth waved from between Genisus's ears as the horse happily rooted out all the treats dangling in front of him. Her other hand held the long reed with the fruits attached. "Guess who's back? I've found reinforcements – of a sort. I assume he belongs to you."

Koorgan stared in disbelief at Ruth. "How did you get up there?" His throat tightened when she started to slip. "Be careful!" he demanded.

She carefully regained her seat. "Do you think I like this? The closest thing to a horse I've ever ridden was at the merry-go-round at the county fair! This thing tried to eat me!" she snapped.

"I'm surprised he didn't," he growled with a fierce scowl. Genisus was now sniffing the end of the reed itself, and began nibbling hopefully.

Ruth held up a small silver object that was too small for him to see clearly from where he was. She looked so tiny compared to the battle steed.

"Yeah, well, just in case you want some trivia: dog whistles work on this beast. Listen, if I can get back down to the reins on this monster, do you think you can use them, and this beast, to pull you up?" she warily asked.

"Yes, but how do you propose untying the reins?" Koorgan reluctantly admitted.

She chuckled. "Hey, give me a little credit here, okay? I've gotten this much done," Ruth stated.

He caught the long reed when she released it and it fell into the hole. He murmured to Genisus when the horse looked down at him and softly neighed. Koorgan weighed the hollow reed in his hand. The only reason Ruth could pick up the long reed had been because it was hollow on the inside.

He had to admire her ingenuity. The reed was at least twenty inches, which must have appeared overwhelmingly huge to her. She had wound some spider web around the end, and then cut up some fruit and twisted the spider web around it to guide Genisus in the direction she wanted his horse to go.

How she had managed to get up on his head without getting herself killed was an incredible feat in itself. He didn't want to think of what could have happened to her if she had been caught in the spider's web, but a shudder ran through him as he imagined the gruesome death. He continued speaking soothingly to Genisus as he watched Ruth carefully negotiate her way down the stallion's mane. His heart was in his throat when he saw her almost fall more than once.

CHAPTER NINE

Ruth clung to a coarse hank of horsehair as she made her way back down to the saddle, her heart wildly beating. Thank god she was strong from lifting weights at the gym every week. Climbing up had been a lot easier and less scary than climbing down! She almost fell when the horse shivered – and then the animal shook his head and stomped his foot.

Ruth released a strangled scream as she swung wildly for a moment, then slid down the mane in an uncontrolled descent. She frantically wrapped her arms and legs around the wiry strands, jerked to a stop, and buried her face against her hands.

"Ruth…," Koorgan quietly called.

"I'm okay – just… just give me a second," she said.

"I will try to keep him calm," Koorgan replied.

She nodded, knowing that he couldn't see her. "That would be nice," she forced out.

Looking down, she gulped for air. "Don't look down, Ruth. That is the first thing the actors in all the movies tell somebody who is terrified of heights, and what do you do? You look down," she chastised.

She focused on reaching the saddle, wrapping a small section of mane around her hand, and moving inch by slow inch until she was lined up with the leather reins. The rueful thought that she could now relate to all the snails, slugs, and sloths in the world ran through her mind.

"I really need a life. If I somehow manage to make it through today without killing myself, I swear I'll work really hard on trying to find one, but just in case some greater power out there hasn't thought of this – I can't do that if I'm dead," she said.

Every one of her muscles was quivering, pushed well past her endurance limits, but adrenaline had kept her going. It felt like she was descending Mount Everest! Of course, the last thing she would have ever thought she would be doing was climbing a prancing, hungry version of this mountain earlier when she had stumbled upon the beast and it had scared the bejesus out of her. The real trick had been finding a way to keep it still while she found a way to get up onto it.

She had tried using the reed, spider web, and fruit first to keep the damn horse still, and it had promptly eaten all three. Her second attempt involved putting a pile of the fruit on a rock. When the horse had reached down to eat the fruit, she had grabbed a handful of the mane that hung down and started climbing with the new reed, spider web, and fruit tied to her purse. The rest was history! Easy! *Not*.

Ruth breathed out a sigh of relief when she reached the saddle where the reins were tied. She was covered in sweat. Droplets of moisture matted her hair down, dripped into her eyes, and stuck her clothes against her skin in unpleasant wet patches. What she wouldn't give for air conditioning right now! She rolled her aching shoulders and released a soft groan at how intensely her muscles were protesting all of her recent activities.

"I am so never going to complain about having too much junk in my purse ever again," she promised herself as she pulled out the box cutter she had used to trim her missing person posters as needed.

She pushed the little silver tab on the side and extended the blade. Reaching down, she held the reins in place as she began to saw through them. After fifteen minutes, she was muttering more than a few choice words about leather, and swearing that she was going to start carrying a blow torch or power saw from now on. It didn't help that the giant in the pit was growing impatient as well.

"Well, have you cut through it yet?" Koorgan demanded.

"Son-of-a-bitch! Did you *have* to use leather for the reins? This stuff is a pain in the butt to try to cut through, you know. Especially with a blade the size of a hair if you were holding it!" Ruth shouted, startling the animal under her. "Oh, crud! Hold on!"

"Genisus! Calm down, boy," Koorgan ordered.

The horse stomped his hoof, but moved to the edge of the hole and looked down. Ruth swallowed as she held on and looked down at Koorgan. She was trying really hard not to cry. She was hot, tired, stressed, and frustrated – not a good combination. And the horse was moseying along again, unwilling to stay still for more than a second if he wasn't focused on eating something.

"Ruth! The rope on my saddle," Koorgan said, his voice filled with hope.

She looked at the thick rope and sighed. "I know, but I can't lift it," she reminded him before her gaze focused on the thin piece of leather holding the rope on the horn of the saddle. "But I can cut through the strap on it more easily than the reins! If he is close enough to the hole, the rope should fall into it," she said as her excitement grew.

Koorgan nodded, looking up at the thick tree branch reaching over the hole. "If you can get me the rope, I can do the rest," he vowed.

Ruth laughed as she moved down to the rope and began cutting on the thinner piece of leather. "Get ready," she called out as she came closer to the other edge of the strap.

Koorgan softly whistled as Ruth sliced through the last bit. The low whistle caused Genisus to move forward quickly and turn along the edge. Ruth's terrified scream mixed with Koorgan's loud curse as she fell along with the rope. She had been caught off guard by the sudden movement of the horse and lost her balance.

Ruth closed her eyes as her life flashed before her eyes. There was so much more that she wanted to do. She braced herself for the harsh impact – and landed on a surprisingly warm surface. Darkness briefly engulfed her and she could feel that she was still in motion, only this time she was cradled on a softer surface than she'd expected. Rolling over onto her side, she curled into a ball, pressed her hands to her eyes, and sobbed.

∼

Koorgan silently cursed as he caught Ruth's falling body between his hands. His fingers wrapped protectively around her as he stepped back into the shadows. His heart pounded and he called himself every kind of a name for his stupidity. He had been so focused on the rope that he hadn't considered that Ruth might not have a good grip on Genisus's mane.

Shaken, he carefully opened his fingers. His breath caught in his throat when he saw her tiny figure lying in the center of his palm, curled into a fetal position. She looked like one of the elusive fairies from the Isle of the Elementals.

He had only heard tales of the mythical kingdom and its residents that floated in the sky, but he could imagine Ruth coming from such a place. Stepping back until his back pressed against the wall of the well, he slid down until he was crouching.

"Ruth. Ruth, do you live?" he murmured.

He reached out a finger to gently touch her, and heard a low moan, followed by a slightly louder curse. He laughed in relief and amusement. This fairy creature had a mouth on her.

He watched as she slowly pushed herself up into a sitting position and ran a hand across her damp eyes. Her hand froze in midair when she realized where she was. Her other hand was pressed to the center of his palm.

His gaze softened when she ran her hand over his skin, pausing the movement as she raised her head and looked around, dazed. Then she looked up at him. Her eyes widened and her mouth dropped open when he raised his hand so that she was eye level with him.

A smile curved his lips when she took in a deep breath, and satisfied that she was alright, he said, "Now, I can properly introduce myself. I am Koorgan, King of the Giants, my Lady." He flashed her a huge smile.

Ruth screamed, it was surprisingly loud for someone of her size, and Koorgan winced. She scrambled back against his curved fingers. He had to cup his hands to make sure that she didn't accidentally fall out of his palms in her terror.

"Holy shit, you are big!" she finally wheezed as she took another deep breath.

"And you, my Lady, are very small," he observed.

"No shit, Einstein," she whispered, looking at him with a wary expression. "Now what?" she asked.

"Now, I get us both out of here," he answered, standing up.

He held her gingerly in his hands, keeping his eyes on her as he moved toward the rope. She was clinging to his finger and her eyes were closed. He was going to need both of his hands to climb out of the hole.

"I'm going to place you in my shirt pocket," he warned.

She opened one eye and peeked up at him before she opened the other and looked at his shirt pocket. She nodded. He moved his hand slowly to his pocket and pulled it open. She peered into it before she looked up at him with an expression of resignation on her face.

"I can't even begin to tell you how humiliating this is," she said, carefully releasing her death grip on his finger so she could sit down on the edge of his hand and slide into his pocket.

"Trust me, being in this hole for two days has been enough humiliation for both of us," he teased.

"That's a long time, especially without a bathroom," she agreed.

She turned and gripped the top of his pocket and looked around the well. He heard her smothered snort. His cheeks flushed with an unexpected warmth when he realized that she had probably noticed the damp section of the wall.

"Hold on," he muttered.

He carefully knelt and tied one of the rocks he had been using to crack open the nuts to the end of the rope before he stood again. He held the coil of rope in his left hand and carefully swung the end with the rock on it in a circle before he released it. The rock soared upward and over the thick branch before falling back into the hole.

"Wow! It looks like you've done that before," she commented.

Koorgan chuckled at her impressed tone of voice. He wished he could see her face. He removed the rock and slipped his booted foot into the loop. He tested the branch to make sure that it could hold his weight before he gripped the other length and began pulling himself up.

"Let me know if I cause you any distress," he said.

"Oh, trust me, I'm enjoying this elevator ride," she replied, her voice amused and… appreciative? Koorgan frowned, but unfortunately, he wasn't in a position to decipher her tone of voice at the moment. He gently swung them back and forth until they were beyond the side of the hole and he could step off into the soft grass.

Genisus trotted over to him. Ruth squealed in alarm when Genisus's inquisitive nose came a little too close to her. Koorgan chuckled, covering his pocket with his hand and turning his body to protect her.

"Easy, Genisus. I'm glad to see you too, boy," he murmured.

He pulled the rope free from the branch and dropped it onto the ground before he gently reached into his pocket. Ruth clung to his finger. He chuckled when she shot him a heated glare without loosening her hold. He walked over and placed her on the limb of a tree where it forked so she could hold onto it.

"It wasn't that funny, you know. You try being the size of an ant and see if some critter as big as an elephant breathing on you doesn't make you want to pee your pants!" she tiredly exaggerated as she gripped the branch and sat down.

He looked at her and nodded. "I imagine it would not be funny. I apologize for offending you. You have indeed proven it is not the size of a person that matters, but the strength of their heart. I don't think I have ever seen such spirit and determination before. You have my undying gratitude, my Lady, for saving me today. I am eternally indebted to you," he said with a bow of his head.

She giggled and waved her hand with a regal gesture as if she were in a pageant. "You can keep kissing up, oh mighty giant. It is kind of empowering at the moment," she commented.

He shook his head and laughed. "As you wish, my Lady," he said with a deep bow.

"Be still my heart. A giant straight from the pages of The Princess Bride," she exclaimed as she fanned herself.

"You are a strange creature, Lady Ruth," he chuckled with a shake of his head. "I have never seen anyone so small."

"Yeah, well, I'm amazing. You may admire me if you must. You know – well, you probably wouldn't know, Mr. King of the Giants, but I've been thinking this might be where Jonathan Swift got his idea for Gulliver's Travels. He was an author on my world – one almost as funny as I am," Ruth said with a wink, leaning back against a leaf.

Koorgan glanced at her while he coiled the rope. "I do not remember ever meeting this man. He is like you?" he asked, stepping up to Genisus and tying the rope back on.

"In the story, yeah, only in reverse. He would have been the giant and you would have been one of the residents of Lilliput. Swift lived like hundreds of years ago. God, I am so tired. Rescuing giants is an exhausting job," Ruth commented, stretching her legs out and yawning.

"I truly am grateful for your rescue, Lady Ruth," Koorgan said.

His gaze softened when he saw her eyes flutter and close for a moment before she forced them open again.

"Hmmm, just wait until you get my bill," she said sleepily. "Though, I could take something in trade. Do you think you can help me find my brother?" she asked, leaning her head to the side, entreating him with her eyes.

Koorgan nodded. "I can send a message to the Isle of Magic on the 'morrow." He stopped and turned when he heard the sound of men's voices growing louder as they approached. He shook his head in disgust and he scowled. "Now he comes!" he snorted.

Ruth sat up and rubbed her eyes. "What now? Oh, God, are you saying there are more of you?" She groaned as several men stepped out of the bushes not far from them, and muttered to herself, "This would have been a lot more fun if I had been the giant."

Koorgan chuckled at her comment and turned to raise his eyebrow at Gant. "Some concerned friend you turned out to be! What took you so long to find me?" he demanded.

Gant shook his head and shot Koorgan a disgusted look. "I've been up all night chasing leads with those damn hounds who couldn't find a flea if it bit them on the ass! How many times do I have to remind you that I can't protect you if I don't know where you are? You said you weren't going to go far! What happened to 'I'm just going for a short ride'? Do you have any idea of the thoughts going through my head when I saw the dead Razor boars and the remains of your crossbow?" he snapped.

Gant paused on the edge of the abandoned well and looked down into the deep hole, frowning ferociously before he jerked his head up to glare at Koorgan. He pointed to the hole.

"Please tell me you didn't fall into that," Gant groaned.

"Very well, I won't tell you. I want it sealed. I'm lucky I didn't break a leg or worse," Koorgan said with a shrug

Gant glanced at the hole again. "How did you get out? It looks pretty deep," he said with a puzzled frown.

"It is. I had a little help," Koorgan replied.

"Ha-ha. Nice pun," Ruth responded with a roll of her eyes, watching warily as the three men who had arrived turned to look at her in surprise.

Gant took a step forward, staring at where Ruth was still sitting. "What is that?" he asked curiously.

"*That* is Lady Ruth," Koorgan introduced. "She rescued me."

"That's me, Ruth the Giant… King… whatever Rescuer," she replied with another yawn. "Listen, this is all very fascinating, but I'd really like to find my brother and get back to where I don't feel like I'm on some bizarre movie set."

Gant looked at Koorgan with a baffled frown. "There are others like her here?" he asked.

"I last saw her brother on the Isle of Magic when we defeated Magna," Koorgan replied, shooting Gant a look of warning.

"Magna! If that creature's family followed the Sea Witch, it would be best to kill her," Gant hissed.

"Whoa, hold on a minute. I think that is a very *bad* idea," Ruth said, standing up and putting her hands on her hips. "First of all, the only connection I have with Magna is that she knew where my brother is and gave me that damn shell with a language issue."

Gant shook his head. "Magna does nothing without a sinister reason.

She is evil. She is responsible for unspeakable atrocities! Entire kingdoms were almost annihilated – every man, woman, and child," he stated.

"She's not evil," Ruth argued, glaring at the man. "Listen, she told me a little of what happened here, and it wasn't her fault. She was taken over by some kind of alien or something. My brother shot her and it gave her and a bunch of other people time to kill the awful thing."

"So she states," Gant retorted.

"Whatever. Unless you want to pay my usual consulting fees, I'm not working out the disputes with your neighbors," she said with a shrug. "I just want to find my brother, wring his neck, and go home."

Gant narrowed his eyes. "The rescuer admits she is a prospective murderess. It is no wonder Magna chose to help you."

"It was a joke!" Ruth spluttered in outrage. "Apparently *your* siblings are perfect little angels? Trust me, mine isn't, but I still love the guy. Mike gave me *rats* for my birthday one year and he's still alive. I would have been justified committing homicide then if I were truly this evil murderess you think I am."

Amusement suddenly lit Gant's eyes as he turned to look back at Koorgan. "She *is* funny," he said with a grin.

Ruth laughed. "Great! I finally find some guys who can appreciate my sense of humor and I can't do a damn thing about it," Ruth grumbled with a sigh.

"Gant, I need you to…," Koorgan started to say when he heard Ruth release a loud shriek. Turning, he caught sight of Ruth being lifted off the branch by a medium size bird. "Ruth!"

"Let me go!" she yelled, struggling to break free as the bird flew higher.

Koorgan, Gant, and the other two men who had been standing silently nearby lunged to catch it. The bird released her with a panicked cry and flew off into the canopy. A long, piercing scream ripped from

Ruth's throat as she fell. Koorgan's eyes followed her trajectory, and he scooped her up before she hit one of the thorny bushes beside the hole. He drew her close, cradling her in his hands.

"Ruth! Ruth, speak to me," Koorgan tenderly demanded, lifting up his hand so he could see her better.

Ruth lay on her back, breathing heavily. "I… am… never… ever… going… skydiving," she whispered in a barely audible voice. "Will you please just close your damn hands over me so I can have a meltdown without everyone looking?" she demanded, lifting her head to glare at him.

A relieved smile curved Koorgan's lips and he nodded. He carefully closed his hands over her, shielding her from Gant and the others. He could feel her body trembling.

He looked at Gant and nodded his head toward the horses. "Get the horses. I am ready to return to the palace," Koorgan instructed.

"Is she going to be alright?" Gant asked, looking with concern at Koorgan.

Koorgan lifted his hand and peeked inside the shelter he had created. Ruth lay on her side with her eyes closed, breathing evenly. Raising his hand to his ear, he could hear the soft sounds of her snores.

"She sleeps. She even makes noise when she does that," Koorgan replied with a grin.

CHAPTER TEN

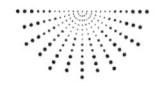

Koorgan carefully cradled Ruth against his chest, trying to keep from shaking her too much on the ride back to the palace. Gant kept giving him an amused look, but he ignored his friend.

"So… are you going to tell me what happened?" Gant finally asked.

He looked at Gant. "What is there to tell? I went for a ride, saw some Razor boar tracks, followed them, and fell in an abandoned well," he said.

"That I had already discerned myself. I'm talking about the… whatever she is you are holding in your hand as if it is a priceless treasure. By the way, may I add this gives a whole new meaning to having a woman in the palm of your hand? Do you think Magna really sent her?" Gant asked.

"Yes, I think Magna sent her. Ruth said she met Magna in her world, and Magna knew her brother. You were with me fighting on the Isle of Magic. You saw the human male who was there," Koorgan replied.

"Yes, I was there. I also saw whatever that alien creature was that Magna was controlling. I am not eager to meet another of her *'friends'*, and in case you hadn't noticed, Mike Hallbrook is of average height," Gant retorted.

Koorgan shook his head. "It was not Magna controlling it, but it controlling Magna. The creature was a parasite. It needed a host body and had taken over Magna's. She had discovered a way to kill it, but she needed help from another world – Ruth's world," Koorgan stated.

Gant shook his head. "How do you know for sure? How do we know that it didn't come from *Ruth's* world in the first place? She could be here to do more damage!" he argued.

Koorgan shot Gant an impatient look. "Nali had a vision about the creature, about its nature and how it arrived – and that it could not be allowed to get near Ashure for some reason. Mike was unique in our fight against the creature because he came from a world without magic, and so did his weapon. Ruth is small right now precisely because Magna gave her a magical artifact that she was not equipped to use. I don't think Ruth or her world had anything to do with the creature," he said.

"Ashure cannot get near the creature? What does the Pirate King have to do with this? Were they afraid he might try to sell the damn thing?" Gant asked.

"Nali didn't say. She only warned that the creature must not get to Ashure. The Empress knows monsters, Gant. While I may not completely trust her, I do believe her. She is not one to exaggerate," he admitted.

"Well, it is a good thing it is dead, then, otherwise Ashure would have it on the auction block," Gant replied.

Koorgan chuckled. "I would have to agree with you," he said.

"You said that Ruth freed you from the pit. If she doesn't have magic, how did she do it?" Gant inquired.

"Determination, ingenuity, and tenacity. She found a reed, covered the end with the web of a spider, and dangled pieces of fruit from the thread. She used the lure to lead Genisus to the hole. Then, she cut the rope from my saddle," he shared with a shake of his head in disbelief.

"How did she get up on Genisus? I'm surprised he didn't try to eat her," Gant replied in a voice filled with admiration.

Koorgan grinned. "She said he did try," he chuckled.

"So, she's a victim of a misused magical artifact – Magna's artifact," Gant said.

"Yes, Ruth said she misspoke the last word of the spell. I have hopes that the spell will wear off. If it doesn't, I will journey to the Isle of Magic and request help from Queen Magika," he stated.

Gant's expression twisted with surprise. "You are ready to open the borders of the Kingdom now that the threat of the Sea Witch has passed?" he asked.

Koorgan frowned. "I have put it off for too long. We worked well with the other Kingdoms to defeat Magna and the alien creature. It would help our Kingdom, especially now that we have a greater supply of products to barter with," he acknowledged.

"Not to mention you won't have to deal with Ashure as much. A little competition will be good for the old pirate," Gant chuckled.

Koorgan laughed as well. "True. It will probably mean more paper-work, though," he glumly added.

"I didn't think of that," Gant replied.

Koorgan took in a deep breath when they emerged from the forest into the meadow. He could see the Palace of Giants on the cliff. He tapped his heels to the stallion's sides and Genisus whinnied before breaking into a gallop.

His thoughts had already turned from the needs of the Kingdom to Ruth. He needed to protect her. A world where everything was so much larger than she was a world of danger. Holding her near to his heart, he knew that whatever magic had brought her to him had done so for a reason. It was a mystery he was determined to solve.

∼

Ruth rolled and stretched. Her hands slid over the soft, silky covers. She felt warm and cozy in her nice little...

"What the heck?" she muttered, sitting up and investigating her new situation.

Her eyes widened when she realized that she was lying on a sponge that was covered in a rectangular piece of pink silk – and her makeshift bed was within a golden birdcage. Beyond the bars, she could see Koorgan's head on a pillow. The cage was on the nightstand next to his bed.

"You have got to be kidding me!" she growled.

At least he didn't hang me from the ceiling, she thought.

Pushing the covers aside, she put her feet on the floor, and saw that someone had removed her boots. She curled her toes in the fluffy rug that covered the metal floor of her cage as she slid out of the bed.

She spied her shoes near the open door of the cage, and slipped them on before she stomped through the door and leaned against the gold bars of the bird cage beside the door. She didn't want to still be inside if he felt like locking her in. Her hand rose to slide along one of the thin bars.

"A golden bird cage? Really? Couldn't you have thought of something a little more original?" she asked sarcastically.

Koorgan rolled over onto his side to face her, stretching out his arm before curling it underneath his pillow.

"You do not like gold?" he asked in a voice still husky with sleep. "I can assure you it was made by the finest craftsmen."

Ruth gripped the bars and gave him her fiercest look. It was the one that warned most of the subcontractors she dealt with to back off or else. When Koorgan chuckled, she figured it didn't seem to work quite as well when she was smaller than a child's Barbie doll.

"This whole golden cage thing is not working for me. Did you send the message to my brother yet?" she demanded, standing up straight and folding her arms across her chest.

Koorgan's smile faded and he scowled at her. "Yes," he said, rolling over and sitting up. "Last night."

"Wait!" Ruth exclaimed before she breathed a sigh of relief when she realized that he was wearing a pair of pajama bottoms. "Thank goodness."

"Thank goodness about what?" Koorgan asked, looking down at her.

"I was afraid that you'd... well, that you'd... you know... sleep in the buff," Ruth said with a blush as she waved her hand at his legs.

Koorgan bent until he was at face level with her. "I normally do," he replied in a deeper voice before he straightened and walked into an adjacent room.

Ruth sank back against the bars and fanned her face. "Holy crap, but that would have been a sight to see," she muttered breathlessly, her eyes glued to his tight ass before he disappeared.

∼

Koorgan juggled the items that started to fall out of the crate that he'd had one of housemaids bring him. He kicked the door to his quarters closed with his foot. A low chuckle escaped him when he thought of the housemaid's expression. Shock was a mild description when he had asked her if she knew where he could obtain some doll furniture, accessories, and clothing. A short time later she had returned with the overflowing crate filled with items.

He carried the items over to his bed. Panic struck him when he saw the cage next to his bed was empty. He frantically searched the floor before he caught a movement out of the corner of his eye.

Ruth was sitting on the edge of the plate that had his partially eaten breakfast. She was eating small pieces of fruit and what looked like crumbs from a muffin. Guilt swept through him that he had not thought to ask her if she was hungry.

"My apologies for not feeding you. I'm afraid I am not doing a very good job of caring for you," he said with a rueful expression.

"Yeah, well, I'm not used to anyone doing the caring part. What's with all the Barbie stuff?" she asked.

"Barbie?" he asked, confused.

"The doll stuff," she said.

He looked down at the crate with a grin. "I have items to make you more comfortable," he replied.

"Really," she said with a raised eyebrow.

He watched her carefully step off the plate and move toward the edge of the nightstand. His throat tightened when she took a running jump onto his bed. He almost dropped the crate when she wobbled before straightening. She crossed the wide bed and motioned for him to set the crate down.

"I need to create a better way for you to move around – one that is not so dangerous," he said, placing the crate on the bed.

"I won't complain. The thought of falling off this damn bed isn't on my list of things to try. If it wasn't for the fact that I was starving, I wouldn't have attempted the journey to the great plate of wonders," she admitted.

"I *will* take better care of you," he muttered.

Ruth laughed. "I'm a big girl, Koorgan. I can take care of myself – well, at least when I'm my normal size. But let's see whose doll house you raided anyway," she quipped.

Koorgan pulled out one item at a time, and Ruth made a running commentary on each piece. He ended up with three piles: items to keep, to give back, and items too hideous to exist. By the time they reached the bottom, she had a new four poster canopy bed with tiny green curtains, a small wooden vanity table that had matching red roses painted on the mirror and chair, a claw-foot bathtub, pedestal sink, toilet – aka fancy chamber pot, a dozen outfits ranging from elaborate dresses to riding outfits, a thimble sized nightstand, and a table with six chairs – though why she needed six was beyond her unless the Lilliputs really did exist out there somewhere and she was expected to entertain them.

"What do you think?" Koorgan asked as he arranged the last piece of furniture in the cage.

"Nice, but we need to figure out a working bathroom – and some kind of wall covering that gives me a little more privacy," she pointed out.

"I'll have the engineers design something today," he assured her.

"Well, thank you, but I'd like to find something a little sooner, if possible," she said with a grimace.

It took a moment for Koorgan to comprehend what she was discreetly trying to say. He stared down at her with panic in his eyes for a moment before he nodded. He reached into the keep pile and picked up the tub, toilet, and sink.

"Ah, perhaps you'd like to pick out some fresh clothing while I set these up," he said, holding up the items and pointing to the bathroom.

"Perfect," she replied with a chuckle.

"I'll be right back," he muttered.

∼

Ten minutes later, Ruth laid back in the tub of hot water on the counter next to the sink. She lifted her foot above the soothing water and wiggled her toes, then leaned her head back and laughed.

"This is totally crazy," she murmured.

Koorgan had fashioned her a miniature bathroom inside his bathroom. Granted, she'd had to use the chamber pot method to use the toilet, but everything else was lovely. Hot water in the tub, a dab of shampoo, a sliver of soap, a towel, and a doll's silk dressing gown had all been laid out for her.

"Is the water warm enough?" he asked.

Ruth squealed and sat up, trying to cover herself with the tiny washcloth. She looked over toward the door with her fiercest 'get-lost' look. He didn't appear to understand her unspoken message.

"Get out! You don't come into the bathroom when a woman is taking a bath!" she hissed with growing alarm when he did just that.

"Why not? You may need my assistance," he said.

"Like what? Washing my back? That would take all of one finger to do!" she retorted.

She warily watched as he lowered the lid on the toilet and sat on it like they – like they were some kind of old married couple! She might have been convinced of his sincerity about her safety if he didn't have that look of amusement in his eyes. Her fists curled in the washcloth. What she wouldn't give to have their positions reversed for just five minutes!

"I would be very gentle," he said in a slightly deeper voice.

"Will you stop that?" she snapped.

"Stop what?" he asked with a raised eyebrow.

"Talking all deep and sexy," she said, mimicking his voice.

He threw his head back and laughed. When he had reined in his chuckles, he looked back at her. "Are you always like this?" he inquired.

"Like... like what?" she stuttered, sitting back when he leaned forward and rested his elbows on his knees.

"Fierce, funny, quick-witted…," he began to list.

She frowned. "Howard would call that being a bitch – but, yes, that's me all the time," she replied.

"Who is Howard?" he growled, his expression changing to a deep frown.

"My ex-husband. He never did understand my sense of humor. I should have married an undertaker. They have better senses of humor than accountants – well, accountants other than me. My problem is I have a sarcastic wit and I'm not afraid to use it. My marriage to Howard lasted all of three miserable years before I looked at him and told him that I liked him alright, but we made better friends than lovers." She released a sharp, self-deprecating laugh. "He quickly agreed. I should have been more suspicious that he was so relieved."

"Why?" Koorgan asked.

Ruth shook her head. "Howard married another accountant the day after our divorce finalized. More power to Betsy. Another year with Howard, and I would have gone mental," she replied with a shrug.

"He is an idiot," Koorgan stated.

Ruth chuckled. "Oh, I agree. Betsy is very high-maintenance. Accountants hate high-maintenance; it kills their balanced budgets," she said.

Koorgan shook his head. "No, he was an idiot not to realize the gem he held within his grasp. I would never let you go if you were mine," he quietly stated.

Ruth blinked when he suddenly stood up. "Call for me when you have finished your bath," he said.

She turned and watched as he exited the bathroom, then sank back in the tub and looked at the water, her mind swirling with conflicting feelings.

"I think that is the nicest thing that anybody has ever said to me," she murmured with a shake of her head.

CHAPTER ELEVEN

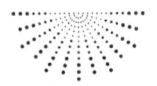

Koorgan ran his hands through his hair as he paced the floor of his bedroom. His attention kept straying back to the bathroom. Curling his fingers into a fist, he called himself every kind of an idiot.

He turned when he heard a knock on the door to his quarters and wavered between staying in his bedroom and answering the door. The decision was quickly made for him when he heard the outer door open and Gant called his name.

"In my bedroom," he called.

He met Gant at the door to his room. Gant cast a critical eye over him before trying to peer behind him. Impatience coursed through him at Gant's curiosity.

"Are you okay? You are acting – a little strangely," Gant carefully informed him.

"Yes, no – Ruth is taking a bath," he replied in a gruff tone.

"A bath? That must be an interesting sight. I hope you plugged the drain or she may end up in a shitload of trouble," Gant said with a snorted laughed at his pun.

"Ha ha," Koorgan said sourly. "I had one of the handmaids bring me a doll's tub. She is relaxing in it," Koorgan snapped.

"Really? Is she – you know – like a real...?" Gant asked, waving his hands up and down his body.

Koorgan shot him a dark look before turning his back to him. He lifted a hand to his face and swallowed as he stared at the door to the bathroom. Gant laid his hand on his shoulder.

"She is all woman," he admitted.

"What is it?" Gant asked.

Koorgan turned back to his friend and confidant. "I don't know," he admitted.

"Well, I have news that you might find interesting," Gant said.

"Have you heard back from the messenger already?" he asked in a sharp voice.

Gant shook his head. "Not yet, but I have heard from some of our merchants. The dragons Magna turned to stone have returned – including Drago's parents. They have returned to their natural form," he shared.

"All of them?" Koorgan demanded.

"I am still reading and confirming the reports. It is as if the evil magic that Magna cast over the Kingdoms is reversing," Gant said.

"Has there been any word...?" Koorgan asked in a tight voice.

"Nay, nothing of your parents," Gant quietly answered.

"Koorgan, I'm ready," Ruth called.

Koorgan immediately turned toward the bathroom door. He paused halfway across the room and turned back to Gant. The man waited with a bemused expression on his face.

"Keep me informed," he instructed.

Gant nodded. "I will. Hello, Lady Ruth," he called out.

"Hello, Gant," Ruth drily replied. "Please tell me there is not a room full of brawny giants in there?"

"Nay, my Lady. Just two, and I am leaving," Gant laughed.

"Thank you for small favors!" she said.

Koorgan shot Gant a fierce look when his friend laughed in amusement. He could feel himself being unreasonably grumpy, but he couldn't seem to help it, and he did not understand why. It just... *bothered* him that Gant found Ruth as fascinating as he did.

He waited until he heard Gant's retreating footsteps in the hall before he entered the bathroom. He stopped at the beautiful sight of Ruth standing next to the tub wearing the silky red dressing gown. Her tiny toes peeked out from under the hem. Her reddish-brown and blonde-streaked hair hung about her shoulders, and for a moment, he wished he could run his fingers through it.

"Koorgan?" she asked, tilting her head to look at him with an inquisitive expression.

He cleared his throat. "I draped a cover over the cage to give you privacy while you dress," he said.

He cupped his hands for her to step onto, raising one finger for her to use to steady herself. She clung to his finger and he swore he could feel the heat of her skin burning through the silk gown. He lifted her to his chest and walked back into his bedroom. Placing her on the nightstand near the cage, he sat down on the bed.

"I'll wait for you to dress. I think it would be best to keep you near me. This way I can keep you safe," he said.

She paused at the entrance to the cage and smiled at him. "Thank you," she said before she disappeared inside the cage that he had covered with a piece of semi-sheer dark blue lace.

He lifted his trembling hands and ran them down his face. What was wrong with him? Dropping his hands to his lap, he stared at the cage. His gut – and his heart – were telling him that his life had just become much, much more complicated, especially when Ruth stepped out a few minutes later and smiled up at him with amusement.

"I have definitely fallen into a fairy tale," she laughed, holding out the skirt of the gown she was wearing before twirling in a circle.

~

Ruth lifted the pinhead size piece of fruit to her lips and took a bite. She stood on a stack of books on Koorgan's desk, reading the document in front of him. Shaking her head, she gave up trying to understand how or why she could understand the strange characters. She finally decided it must have been part of the spell from the shell. After all, she could also understand what Koorgan, Gant, and all the others she had encountered were saying.

"Tell them 'no' on the lumber agreement. The amount they are demanding for the amounts they are willing to pay is ridiculous. Not only that, they have a clause that states they get an exclusive contract, yet if you look at the third paragraph, they are charging you an import fee that will reduce your profit margins by another three percent. Who are these jerks?" Ruth asked with a shake of her head.

Koorgan looked over at her with a surprised expression on his face. "Pirates. You actually understand this – stuff?" he inquired.

Ruth laughed. "I eat this stuff up for breakfast, lunch, and dinner. Mike said it was because it always gave me someone to fight with. I like getting a fair deal and I'm not afraid to fight for it. Trade agreements, economics, and accounting are like playing a great game of chess; you always have to think several moves ahead of your opponent," she explained.

Koorgan sat back in his chair. "Are you saying that you enjoy reading these types of documents?" he asked with an incredulous expression.

"Yes, I enjoy it," she laughed.

"I would like to learn this game of chess," Koorgan said, leaning forward and resting his chin on his palm.

"I can show you how it's done," she cheekily replied.

He reached out and caressed her cheek with his fingertip before dropping his hand onto the book beside her. "I wish there was a way to make you grow," he admitted.

"Me too," she sighed. "There's a story in my world called Alice's Adventures in Wonderland," she said, leaning back and kicking her feet.

Ruth ran her hand over his finger, her mind working on remembering the details of the story. It had never been one of her favorites. For some reason, the story and the subsequent movie had always freaked her out.

"Alice was a young human girl who followed a white rabbit and fell into a strange world. Silly girl. The bunny could have had rabies for all she knew, but Alice didn't think of that. Well, the author didn't think of adding that little cautionary detail. Personally, I think the 'white rabbit' was code for whatever he was smoking. Anyway, Alice found two different types of food – I can't remember what it was – but if she ate one, she shrank and if she ate the other, she grew," Ruth explained, sitting up to brush her bangs out of her eyes with one hand.

Koorgan's eyes widened before they glittered with determination. He suddenly grinned and stood up. Ruth clumsily climbed back to her feet.

"That's it!" he exclaimed.

"What's it?" Ruth asked in exasperation as Koorgan walked over to the door, opened it, and spoke to someone on the other side.

"Get me the Director of Archives," Koorgan ordered.

A few minutes later, an elderly man with long gray hair and a neatly trimmed goatee stepped into the room. He glanced curiously around before his startled gaze froze on her. She smiled and waved to him after he rubbed his eyes and looked at her again.

Ruth listened to Koorgan as he spoke at a rapid clip to the man about mushrooms. The gray-haired man nodded, looked her way, and nodded again before he turned and hurriedly exited the room.

Could it be that they actually have magical food like in Alice's Wonderland? Just how many authors from my world got their ideas from the Seven Kingdoms? Maybe everyone *who smokes hallucinogens ends up here,* she thought incredulously.

She turned and slid down off the books, then walked over to the edge of his desk and looked up at him with excitement.

"What's going on?" she asked when he returned to his seat.

"A possible solution to both of our problems, my little rescuer," Koorgan replied with a mysterious smile. "Now, about this agreement."

Ruth looked at Koorgan suspiciously for a moment before she sighed and turned back to the paper lying on his desk.

Do not get your hopes up, Ruth! Don't do it, she told herself, and forced her attention back to the contract.

∼

A week later, Koorgan moodily stood on the terrace outside of his office gazing out over the Kingdom. His fingers curled on the stone railing. Below him, he could see the city and the harbor.

"What are you so lost in thought about? Another contract? A decision about who gets the chickens and who gets the cow?" Gant teased, walking up to stand beside him.

"Nay," Koorgan distractedly answered.

"Where is Ruth?" Gant asked, turning to look through the doors into the office.

"She said I was too much of a distraction and told me to take a break," Koorgan replied.

"Ah… So, still no change," Gant murmured.

"Nay," Koorgan replied.

"Has Gerryman found anything that may help?" Gant inquired.

Koorgan shook his head. "Nay. He has searched all of the archives. I was confident the mushrooms would restore Ruth back to her normal size," he said.

"What of Queen Magika? Surely, she or King Oray would know of a reversal spell," Gant said.

"Nay again. She has sent word to the witch's village where Ruth's brother lives, but all she said about Ruth's situation is that a miscast spell can have unusual consequences. Without knowing the exact spell and the power behind it, she said it is difficult to know how long the spell may last or how to unravel it. Only the witch who created the spell has the power to undo it," Koorgan replied.

Gant cursed softly. "It isn't likely that Magna will suddenly appear and offer her assistance," he muttered.

Koorgan nodded. "I know," he growled in frustration.

"You care about her, don't you?" Gant prodded.

Koorgan glanced at Gant before turning his back and walking along the balcony. He could sense Gant following him – waiting for an answer that he suspected his friend already knew. His expression softened when he looked through the window at his desk. Ruth was holding the pen as if it were a lover, moving it along the parchment contract and muttering to herself, her expressive face changing from outraged to amused.

In the past week, he had learned so much about her. They spent every waking moment together – and every night. He would lay in his bed and she in hers, and they would talk for hours. She fed his desires in so many different ways.

He loved her smart-mouthed comments, her inquiring mind, her beauty, and the pure heart beneath. He had laughed more in the past week than he had...in his entire life. The way she growled at him sometimes when he dared her to get angry, her eyes sparkling just before she gave him an iron-clad rebuttal that had him marveling at her cleverness... he ached to touch her as a man touched a woman.

One of his favorite times of the day was waking in the morning before her and watching her sleep. She liked to sleep on her right side with her arms around a pillow. Her delicate eyelashes lay like crescents against her freckled cheeks.

"Koorgan, are you alright?" Gant asked.

He nodded and released a deep sigh. "Yes to both of your questions. I am falling in love with her, Gant. I've never met a woman like her before. She challenges me. I can talk to her about anything. If she doesn't agree with me, she explains why and argues her point with logic and passion. It is as if she can see me as a man without all of the trappings of my wealth and power," he shared.

Gant placed his hand on Koorgan's shoulder, and Koorgan looked over into his friend's concerned eyes. He bowed his head in appreciation, glad to be understood, to be cared for. Their friendship was truly one of the things Koorgan treasured most.

"Then we will find a way to break the cursed spell Ruth is under – even if it means bringing Magna back to do it," Gant vowed.

Koorgan chuckled. "I have already been thinking about that," he admitted.

"I'll work on it as a backup plan," Gant said, dropping his hand. He looked through the window at Ruth. "I will confess that I envy you, Koorgan," Gant admitted, a note of longing in his voice. Then he continued more gruffly. "If there is any way to break the curse, it will be done."

Koorgan turned and watched Gant stride down the balcony. He returned his attention to Ruth. She was the only woman that he'd ever had this type of deep attraction to. He rubbed his hand over his heart as he watched her quietly work. The magic of the giant's mushroom, one of the few that still remained from the spreading blight, had not changed her as he had hoped. He feared nothing would, and he would be destined to love her as they were.

CHAPTER TWELVE

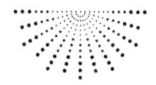

"Close your eyes," Koorgan softly instructed her.

"Why? Are you going to get naked?" she teased.

"I would be very happy to do so if you so wish, my Lady," he growled with a chuckle.

Ruth bit her lip and laughed. "I think I might actually faint at the sight of so much manly goodness," she joked breathily, her cheeks flushing.

His warm breath swept over her, his eyes dancing with amusement at her reaction. She fanned herself with her hand, trying to cool the sudden heat flooding her body as she remembered the few glimpses of flesh and morning arousal she had seen over the past week. It wasn't her fault she'd seen just enough to make her imagination really soar.

If only..., she wistfully thought.

He motioned for her to cover her eyes and she did. They had been out and about all morning – if you could call walking the halls and being in his office working 'being out'. She had loved it when he took her on a tour of the castle after a morning filled with contracts, document reviews, and meetings about economic development.

"You can open them now," he whispered near her ear.

Ruth opened her eyes. Her breath caught and she took a step forward on his hand. Her arm wrapped around his finger.

"Oh my God, are you serious?" she breathed.

His nightstand had been replaced with a larger version, and sitting in the middle of it was a beautiful replica of the castle – and it was the perfect size for her. He walked forward and placed her on the cobbled path that led to the front gates. Unable to resist, she stepped over to the grass and bent to run her hand along it.

"It feels so real," she said in wonder.

Koorgan smiled. "It is. It is a moss that grows close to the ground," he explained.

Her gaze moved to the flower beds with tiny, delicate flowers blooming. Lifting her skirt, she walked to them and gently rubbed a petal between her fingers. "And these…," she inquired, looking at him.

Koorgan pulled up a chair and sat down next to the long chest. "They look full grown to you, but they are small wildflowers that grow that size. They have been enchanted to remain like that," he said.

"Oh, this….," she waved her hand to the palace.

"The finest craftsmen in the Kingdom have been working day and night on this for you," he explained.

Ruth chuckled and shook her head. "The bill for this thing is going to put a small dent in your treasury! I was doing okay with the golden bird cage," she said.

"You don't like it?" he asked.

Ruth saw the swift disappointment in his eyes. "No – no, I love it! I just worry that you spent so much… for me," she lamely finished.

Koorgan lowered his head until his chin was even with her. "I would do so much more for you if I could, Lady Ruth," he said.

Ruth looked at him with a bemused expression. "You're doing it again," she murmured.

"Doing what?" he asked.

She waved her hand in a circle. "That – that deep voice thing that turns me... Oh, hell," she muttered.

Walking across to him, she placed her hands on his lips and leaned forward. She kissed his bottom lip, then she stepped back far enough that she could look up at him without him going cross-eyed.

"Thank you," she said.

He sat back and gazed down at her with a soft expression. "Go explore. Everything works. You have running water, lights, a bathroom, anything that my craftsmen could imagine. They did this for you, my Lady, not for me," he said.

"Why? They don't even know me," she said.

"You saved their King, Ruth. Everyone in the Kingdom has heard of your remarkable feat," he explained.

"Oh."

That was the only thing she could think of to say in response. What did you say when you were given a castle? She walked along the path to the front steps. Lifting her skirt in both hands, she slowly climbed them and stepped through the open door.

Her eyes burned at the beauty of the interior. The craftsmen had lovingly focused on each minute detail from the marble floors to the delicate woodwork. Stained glass windows provided light and privacy on the ground floor.

Her hand caressed the beautiful wood of the grand staircase as she climbed the stairs. At the top, she found herself in a gorgeous dining room. Four chairs surrounded a small round table. To the right was a sitting room with plush seating. Ornate decorations lined the high ceiling. A decorative mural was carved around the hanging chandelier.

She turned in a circle, trying to take everything in. Then she stepped into a two-story library. A grand piano sat to the side. She walked over and ran her fingers across the keyboard, astonished when musical notes rang out. There were several chairs and lamps set in front of a large fireplace with a filigree brass fire screen.

Ruth walked over to one of the bookshelves. Her hand ran down along the volumes before she pulled one out and opened it. Her mouth dropped open when she saw that it was a complete volume. She selected several more books. Each volume was a readable story. She carefully replaced them.

Ruth spent the next hour exploring her new home. On the ground floor, she found the kitchen complete with a magical fireplace and working stove, sink, and ice box. On the third floor she found the master bedroom which looked just like the one they were in. She finally walked out onto an open garden just outside the master bedroom, and stopped when she saw the table laid out and a tiny candle burning.

"Koorgan…," she said, looking up at him with tears in her eyes.

"Would you have dinner with me, my Lady?" he asked.

She lifted a hand and wiped the tear that escaped from her cheek. "You are crazy, but yes, I'd love to have dinner with you," she said.

He chuckled and pulled a chair out for her. Ruth walked over and sat down. He lifted the silver cover from her plate and expertly poured a drop of wine into her goblet. She looked at him with an amused grin.

"You're pretty good at this. You didn't happen to play with dolls when you were a kid, did you?" she asked in a light tone.

"I will never tell, my Lady," he said with a grin, lifting his glass of wine.

Ruth laughed and lifted her goblet. "Thank you," she said, sipping her wine.

"No thanks are ever needed, my Lady," he said.

Ruth picked up her fork and waved it at him. "You're doing that voice thing again that drives me crazy. You better be thankful there is a little bit of a size difference at the moment or I'd be saying to hell with dinner and let's get to the dessert," she joked.

"And I would take you up on it," he promised.

Ruth's hand paused in midair. She slowly lowered it back to her plate. The smile on her lips faded.

"We can't do this, Koorgan," she said, staring across at him.

"We cannot stop what has already begun, Ruth. I want to know more about you. I want to spend time with you," he stated.

"But what if…," she started to say before she looked down at her plate.

"Then we will deal with it," he vowed.

She picked up her glass of wine and took another sip. Her mind was going around in circles. Their teasing had led to something different and she wasn't sure she was ready to deal with the discussion.

Hell, she hadn't had a serious relationship since Howard! After her parents' sudden illnesses and deaths, she had been working on one extensive forensic audit case after another. Demand for her expertise was growing as she took on the more high-profile cases. Mike's disappearance had made her realize that she had buried herself in her work to ignore the emptiness in her life.

"What is your favorite color?" Koorgan suddenly asked.

Ruth looked up and blinked. "My favorite color? I – blue, I guess. It reminds me of the ocean and the sky on a beautiful day. What is your favorite color?" she asked in return.

"It is mine as well, though green comes in a close second," Koorgan answered.

For the next hour, they chatted about their favorite things and the things they absolutely hated. They had moved from their respective dinner tables to the giant-sized garden outside so they could watch the sunset. She sat on a swing hanging from the branch of a decorative tree while he sat on the bench next to her. Ruth laughed when Koorgan mentioned his distaste for spiders and mussels. She agreed with him – neither were favorites of hers either.

"And rats! Mike gave me rats for my sixteenth birthday because he heard they made good pets. I ended up with a million of the damn things! I never knew they could reproduce so quickly," she shared.

∼

Later that evening, Ruth finished brushing her hair out and placed the brush on the vanity table in her new bedroom. Her eyes kept moving to the open balcony doors of her new house.

"Ruth, are you still awake?" Koorgan inquired.

"Yes, you can open the panel," she answered.

She stood up and ran her hands down along the silk dressing gown that covered the delicate nightgown Koorgan had given her earlier in the day. Her gaze moved to the row of elegant clothing hanging in the small armoire, then she looked up when the wall of her room slowly opened.

"You don't mind if I keep this open, do you? I feel better being able to see you," he said.

She swallowed and shook her head. "No, not at all. It is kind of neat living in a castle with moving walls, almost like being at Hogwarts. Did you know that there are actual hidden passages in this place? I found one by accident when I went to get a book out of the library," she nervously laughed.

"The castle is an exact replica of this one. I wanted you to be able to explore anywhere in it. Gant and I used to play in the hidden passages when we were children," he replied.

"Mike and I would have loved to have something like that when we were kids. We had refrigerator boxes," she said, laughing at the memory.

"He and Marina are on their way here," he shared.

Ruth stepped forward in surprise. "When will they arrive?"

Koorgan lifted his hand for her to step onto his palm. She clung to his finger as he carried her over to his bed, then stepped down when he rested his hand on his pillow. She turned to sit on the pillow while he climbed onto the bed and laid down.

"Ashure offered to bring them. It can take anywhere from a day to a week depending on his mood. On a positive note, Marina is a powerful enough witch and can literally create a fire under his ass if he procrastinates too much," he said.

"I haven't even met this guy yet and I'm not sure I like him," she growled.

Koorgan laughed. "Stand in line. Honestly, Ashure is not so bad. He just has this charming personality that makes everyone want to kill him," he jested.

She laid back on his pillow and yawned. "Okay. As long as I'm not alone in feeling this way, there are more suspects and I can always create an iron clad alibi. I've watched enough NCIS episodes to avoid the plot holes," she quipped in return.

They both fell silent and stared up at the ceiling. Soon, her eyes grew heavy. The great food, wine, hot bath, and the miles – comparable to her size, anyway – that she'd walked as she explored the miniature castle had worn her out. Turning onto her side, she yawned and reached for the pillow she normally snuggled. Instead of a pillow, she wrapped her arms around Koorgan's little finger. She rubbed her cheek against his finger and released a long sigh.

"Ruth," he murmured.

"I'm just going to rest my eyes for a minute," she replied in a voice heavy with exhaustion.

Koorgan lay on his side and watched Ruth's eyelashes flutter until they rested upon her cheeks. She had both of her arms wrapped around his little finger and her cheek resting against it. A small smile of amusement curved his lips when she released a soft snore.

He lay there until he felt sleep pulling at him, too. Afraid to leave her next to him for fear of rolling over and crushing her, he gently slid his hand under her body and cradled her in his hand. Sliding out of his bed, he stood up and carefully placed her in her own miniature bed.

"Sweet dreams, my beautiful Ruth," he murmured, pulling the cover over her.

Koorgan returned to his bed and lay on his back with one arm under his head. He would speak with Marina. She had opened a portal between their world and Mike's, not once, but twice. It was possible that she could do it again. If she could, then he had a quest for Gant. His head turned and he looked over at Ruth.

"We will be together, Ruth. I swear it," he quietly promised.

CHAPTER THIRTEEN

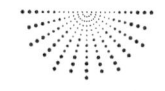

"Oh my God! Ruth? What the hell happened to you?" Mike exclaimed.

Ruth shot a confused look at Koorgan. He gave her an apologetic smile and bent closer to her. She could feel Mike's stunned eyes still locked on her.

"I might not have mentioned that you were smaller than he remembered," Koorgan murmured.

Ruth rolled her eyes at Koorgan before she turned her attention back to her brother. He was standing next to a very obviously pregnant young woman who was staring at her curiously. It was very clear that she wasn't as shocked as Mike was, but then again, she had never met Ruth when she was their size.

"What do you think happened to me, Sherlock? This is what happens when you disappear and I try to find your ass! What were you thinking just disappearing like that? Are you nuts? We're family, Mike. You don't leave family like that," Ruth snapped before her voice broke.

"Ah, hell. Don't cry. You know I can't stand it when you cry," Mike murmured.

"I never cry," she sniffed.

Mike crossed the room and bent down on one knee so he could look at her. He lifted his hand toward her and paused. She stepped forward, grabbed his finger, and hugged him.

"I'm so sorry, Ruth. I never meant for any of this to happen," he said in a low voice.

Ruth nodded. "I know. Neither did I. I'm just glad you are alright," she replied.

He carefully pulled his hand away and stood up. He held his hand out to the young woman who had been silently watching them. She stepped forward with a smile.

"This is Marina, my wife," he introduced.

Ruth rubbed a hand across her cheek and smiled back at the woman. "Hi Marina. I'm Ruth, Mike's big sister," she greeted.

Marina laughed when Mike released a smothered groan. Ruth grinned at her.

Marina looked at Mike. "I like her," Marina stated.

"They are going to conspire together, I just know it," Mike bemoaned, pulling Marina into his arms and pressing a kiss to her lips.

"You're damn right we are – once I'm back to my normal self," Ruth grudgingly added.

"I agree. Now will you tell me what in the hell is going on?" Mike demanded.

~

She hadn't really thought about it until Mike and Marina's arrival earlier today, but she'd been here with her giant for a month now. She looked up as Koorgan came into their bedroom. That was another thing she had gotten used to – being with Koorgan.

He smiled down at her with that sexy, half-smile of his that drove her nuts. Over the past month, she had realized something else that had scared the shit out of her – she was falling in love with the giant and she didn't have a clue what to do about it. She gripped the pillowcase as he carefully slid into bed. Even as gentle as he was, the movement still almost sent her toppling.

"What are you thinking about?" Koorgan asked, lying on his side next to her.

She laid down and rolled over to face him. "That life is never as simple as you hope it might be. What am I going to do? I can't go home like this. Even if I wasn't this small, what do I have to go home to? A job? An empty house? Mike's life is here now. He was all I had back home," she murmured.

"Then stay here," Koorgan replied in a soothing voice, reaching out so that she could touch his finger. "Stay with me."

Ruth sniffed and pulled Koorgan's finger down so she could hug it to her. It was the only contact they could really have, and it was breaking her heart.

"And what? Live in the dollhouse next to your bed for the rest of our lives? What kind of life is that for either of us?" she asked in a thick tone.

"It is better than no life at all without you. Sleep, my precious Ruth. We will find a way to be together," Koorgan said in a gruff voice.

Ruth pressed a kiss to his finger before letting it go. She sat up and slid down the pillow. He leaned up on his elbow to watch her walk across the bed to the small bridge he had connected to the nightstand. She turned on the bridge and gave him a sad smile.

"Goodnight, Koorgan," she said.

"Sweet dreams, my Ruth," Koorgan replied, lying back against the pillow.

Ruth could feel his eyes on her as she crossed the bridge to the path and made her way up the staircase to the master bedroom in the dollhouse. She smiled at him again as she removed her silk robe and slippers before she pulled back the covers and climbed into bed. She reached over and turned off the lamp on the nightstand. Only when she had laid back down did he reach over and turn off the light next to him.

Moonlight lit the bedroom through the open doors. The scent of the ocean floated on the light breeze that came in through the open French doors. The sheer curtains danced like ghostly lovers reaching for each other.

A tear coursed down from the corner of her eye. Ruth rolled over and reached for the pillow to cuddle it. She frowned when her hand touched something hard and smooth. She picked up the item, exploring it in the dark. Holding it in the faint light of the moon, she realized it was the magic shell Magna had given her. She thought she had lost it when she was in the forest, but it must have been in her purse the entire time, then fell out into the bed at some point. She knew she needed to clean that thing out.

She held it up to her ear, gleefully shocked when she heard the faint sound of a word. She closed her eyes and made a silent wish before she whispered the word. She waited to see if anything would happen. Disappointment washed through her when nothing transpired.

Ruth rolled onto her side and lay the shell inside the small jewelry box on her nightstand. She stared at it for over an hour before she realized that she just couldn't sleep. She turned and stared at Koorgan's relaxed face with longing. For just one night, she would give anything to be next to him.

"Oh, hell. Just do it, Ruth! Live a little bit on the dangerous side. What is the worst thing that could happen? Okay, don't think of the worst thing that can happen, otherwise you won't do this," Ruth muttered, pushing the covers back and sliding out of her lonely bed.

She picked up her dressing gown and slipped her slippers back on. Exiting her room, she silently descended the staircase. Minutes later, she had retraced her steps back to Koorgan's bed. She climbed over the rumpled bedcovers and up onto the pillow that she often sat on. She reached out and touched the soft strands of his dark brown hair.

His eyes are the same beautiful dark brown, she reflected as she stepped back and sank down on the pillow. She sat and watched him sleep.

Her mind replayed the word she heard in the shell. It meant 'wish'…. She didn't know why she understood the word now. Maybe she had to be here to understand the language. Why would the shell give her this word now? Was it still part of the magic contained in the shell? Or worse, had it just been her imagination?

"I wish I could stay with you," she whispered in the darkness.

The tears that had burned her eyes earlier returned and she laid down on the pillow, tucking her hands under her cheek. She continued to watch Koorgan sleep until her eyes grew heavy and she couldn't keep them open any longer. A soft sigh slipped from her as she fell into a deep, dreamless sleep.

∼

Koorgan woke suddenly when he felt a warm hand slide across his bare abdomen. An equally warm body was pressed firmly against his back. Anger flared inside him that any woman would dare enter his sleeping chambers without his permission, much less his bed without an invitation.

He reached down and gripped the hand that had been moving down to the waistband of his sleeping trousers. A low, sleepy murmur brushed against his ear, and his hand froze. He carefully turned until he was facing his bed companion.

His breath caught in his throat when he saw Ruth's delicate head lying on the pillow beside him. The hand that had been wrapped around his body moved to lie on his hip. He gently caressed her cheek.

She released a soft moan and snuggled closer to him. He didn't know what had happened during the night – what magic had transpired –

but he was thankful. Ruth was in his bed, in his arms, and she was full size. She sighed in her sleep and rolled onto her back, throwing one arm up over her head. Leaning closer, he pressed a light kiss near her ear.

"Ruth, my love, wake up," he murmured next to her ear.

CHAPTER FOURTEEN

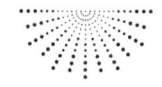

"Ruth, my love, wake up."

Ruth groaned and tried to roll over, but something warm and heavy was preventing her from moving. It was too early to wake up. She had never been the best morning person, even if her career meant she needed to be at times. Fortunately, most of what she did as a consultant didn't start until after a pot of coffee had been drunk and most of the rush hour traffic was in full swing.

"Five more minutes," she mumbled, refusing to open her eyes.

A soft chuckle sounded in her ear, and then she felt the warmth of lips along her neck. The all too realistic sensation enticed her from the ardent, scorching dream that she'd been having. Her hands immediately rose up in alarm and she froze when they encountered hot, well-muscled flesh. Taking in a deep breath, she slowly opened her eyes, and… screamed.

"Ouch! That is not the type of morning greeting I was hoping for," Koorgan chuckled, pulling back to rub his ringing ear.

Ruth's throat worked up and down as she tried to speak, her shocked eyes locked with Koorgan's amused brown ones. He was staring back at her like she was….

"You've shrunk," she whispered in a hoarse voice.

Koorgan shook his head. "You've grown," he replied, leaning back down over her. "I don't know how, but I won't complain."

Ruth started to turn her head to look at the dollhouse that had been her home, but Koorgan gently guided her chin back toward him. Her lips clamped shut when he pressed a kiss to them. He leaned back when she refused to part her lips.

"You do not want my kiss?" he asked.

Ruth shook her head, then paused, and nodded. She finally sighed, and tenderly touched his cheek.

"Morning breath. I need to freshen up, then we can kiss," she replied with a self-conscious grin.

Koorgan laughed and hugged her to him before he rolled to the other side of the bed and stood up. Ruth admired the way his muscles flexed as he moved, his bare chest, his morning shadow of whiskers, and his early morning hard-on.

Holy cow, he has one hell of a body!

Koorgan smiled down at her with an intense expression. "If you keep looking at me like that, I won't give a damn about your fear of morning breath. If you wish to freshen up, I suggest you do so now because, either way, I fully intend to take you as mine," he warned her.

Ruth grinned back at him. "Wow! You are definitely my kind of guy," she murmured.

She reached out to grip his hand. A shiver ran through her and she swallowed as her feet sank into the thick rug next to the bed and she stood up. Koorgan was still at least a head taller than she was, but it was a hell of a lot better than it had been the previous month!

She reached out and slid her hands over the silky flesh of his taut stomach, then his chest. She paused on his man boobs. His nipples were hard and his chest was covered with just enough hair that she could slide her fingers into it and…

"I do not think your breath is bad," Koorgan grumbled and pulled her closer so she could feel his desire. "I can kiss the rest of you instead if you would like."

Her eyes lifted to meet his. Wonder filled her. She didn't know if it was the magic of the miniature shell or if the spell had worn off, but she hoped that whatever had happened last night never disappeared.

"I think that is an excellent idea," she murmured, sliding her hand back down his stomach and over the front of his pants. "How about we take turns?"

"How about we get back in bed?" Koorgan asked with a wicked grin.

Ruth tilted her head and laughed. "How about we take this to the shower? I've always wanted to try that. Then we can try the bed," she suggested with a mischievous look.

She released a startled squeak when Koorgan suddenly scooped her up in his arms. She wrapped her arm around his neck and clung to him as he strode across to the elegant bathroom. Turning her face in to his neck, she pressed hot, little kisses all along the thick column. For the past month, she had fantasized about all the things she wanted to do to him. Come hell or high water, she was going to do them all – over and over and over again!

"The shower and then the bed," he agreed.

Ruth ran her hands down over Koorgan's shoulders as he placed her back on her feet, unable to believe any of this was real. Leaning forward, she pressed her lips against his shoulder. He felt real. He tasted real, but she was still terrified that it was all just a dream.

He opened the large clear door of the shower and turned on the water. Her fingers undid the tie of her dressing gown and he pushed it off her shoulders. His fingers slid under to the straps of her gown and he pushed them off of her shoulders. The soft material pooled around her feet, leaving her bare since she had not been wearing any panties.

She heard his swift intake of breath and gave him a sexy, knowing smile. Her hands slid down his chest to his stomach before she ran her fingers along the waistband of his pants. She gathered up the material between her fingers and she slowly pushed them down.

She kept her eyes locked on his face. "I am so looking forward to kissing you all over," she breathed out as the material fell around his ankles. "Every succulent inch of you."

"Goddess, Ruth! You have no idea how much I have dreamed of this moment," Koorgan groaned.

He stepped into the shower as she moved closer. A wild, wicked pleasure swept through her and she knew that her bad side had taken control. At the moment, she was feeling very, very naughty in a very, very good way.

"Oh, baby, you haven't seen anything yet!" Ruth assured him with a glimmer of determination that promised ecstasy as she wrapped her hand around his cock and began massaging him.

"Sweet heavens," Koorgan's loud groan echoed throughout the bathroom when Ruth knelt down and started kissing where her hands were.

~

The feel of Ruth's hands and lips running down his body sent even more of his blood rushing straight to his cock. His eyes remained locked on her as she explored him, brushing her fingers over his skin, and then she followed the exploration with her lips. She grazed his hip and he saw her tongue come out to swipe the droplets of water.

"Goddess, Ruth, you are so beautiful," he murmured.

His hands trembled as he rested them on her shoulders before he slid them along her skin up to her hair. He bent forward to protect her eyes from the water when she looked up at him and smiled. Her eyes glowed with warmth – and a deeper emotion.

"Hand me the soap," she requested.

He reluctantly released her so that he could hand her the bar of soap. She reached up with one hand. A low moan slipped from him when she released his cock to lather her hands.

With meticulous care, she began lathering his body. He pressed his hands against the tile of the shower to keep from grabbing her and burying his throbbing cock inside her. He knew that she wanted this time to learn more about him on an intimate level.

Her hands ran up and down his legs. He tilted his head back and gritted his teeth when her hand slid all the way up the inside of his thigh to cup his heavy sack. She rolled his balls gently between her palms before she caressed the spot under them.

"No more," he gritted out.

"Lots more. Don't forget you are a giant. I have a lot of ground to explore," she teased.

"I… Goddess, don't stop," he moaned.

Her soapy hand was now moving back and forth along his cock, pumping it from base to tip in an erotic movement that had his hips rocking with her strokes. His fingers curled into twin fists and he looked down so he could watch her. He couldn't wait until it was his turn to torture her.

She was merciless in her exploration. Her slick, soapy hands ran over every inch of his body, front and back. When she was done, she rubbed her breasts against his back, moving in the same calculated rhythm as her hand as she once again pumped his cock.

He desperately needed her. Pre-cum mixed with the water from the shower and he knew that when he took her this first time, it would not be long before he came. Her hands slid around his body and she ducked under his arm so she could stand in front of him.

"Your turn," she whispered, gazing up at him with desire-ladened eyes.

"I hope you are not going to ask me for mercy," he warned in a strained voice.

Her lips twitched. "If I do, I hope you ignore me," she replied.

"Only until you scream with pleasure," he swore.

He took the soap and lathered his hands. Unlike her, he started at the top. He had plans as he worked his way down. He captured her lips and deepened the kiss.

Their tongues danced, fought, and surrendered to each other. Her fingers curled on his shoulders as his hands began to move over her. He caressed the sensitive spots along her throat and down over her shoulders. He pulled her closer and ran his large hands across her shoulder blades and down along her spine to the curve of her ass.

His hands tightened on her buttocks and he pulled her against his throbbing cock so that she could feel how much he wanted her. Her muffled gasp told him that she was very aware of his raging desire. He continued to kiss her as he ran his fingers along the tantalizing crack of her ass.

He kept one hand against her buttock as he moved the other around and down between her legs. She moaned and wiggled against him. He gripped his heavy cock and rubbed it against her swollen mound.

Ruth broke their kiss and pressed her face against his shoulder. "Koorgan, please," she moaned.

He could feel her body rocking. "What do you want, Ruth?" he murmured.

"I want to come. I want to feel you buried so damn deep inside me that you could plant a forest with the seed you'll spill," she panted.

He chuckled at her analogy. He planned on planting himself deep inside her and spilling a lot of seed – over and over. The vivid image caused his cock to jerk and he could feel more precum coating the tip. If he wasn't careful, his revenge for her torture could backfire on him.

He lifted his hands and cupped her breasts. Bending down, he captured her taut nipple between his lips and sucked until it was throbbing and plump. He did the same to the other. Once they were both swollen from his attention, he captured them between his fingers in a firm grasp that caused her back to bow toward him.

"Holy Cow! I didn't realize they could be so sensitive," she groaned. "Harder… Oh, yeah."

Her hips were moving and her eyes were closed. A low curse slipped from him. There was only so much torture a man could take and what he was doing with Ruth was killing him after encouraging her explorations.

He straightened, captured her lips in a hard, fierce kiss, and turned off the water. She blinked up at him in a daze. He stepped out of the shower, pulling her behind him. Grabbing the towel, he wrapped it around her and lifted her into his arms.

"What are you doing?" she asked in confusion.

He glanced down at her as he carried her out of the bathroom to his bed. "I'm going to fuck you," he said in a tight voice.

"But… we'll get your bed wet," she stammered.

"Oh, it is going to be very wet by the time I get done with you," he vowed.

Her lips parted into the shape of an 'O'. She wrapped her arms around his neck and pulled his head down to capture his lips. They tumbled onto the bed in a frenzy of passion. Her legs parted and she wrapped them around the back of his thighs.

Koorgan was beyond playing around now. They could do that later. He rose far enough to align himself with her welcoming depths. With a primal, desperate need, he impaled himself in one fluid stroke – burying himself as deep as he could.

"Yessss!" Ruth groaned.

Koorgan felt her body arch up against his and her fingers dug into his forearms as her sweet, warm feminine core wrapped around his cock. He barely gave her body time to adjust to his engorged shaft before he gritted his teeth and pulled almost all the way out. Her hands and legs tightened on him and her eyes opened with desperate need.

He pushed forward, filling her again. Lowering his body almost flat against hers, he wrapped his arms around her and held her tightly as they began to move in unison, pushing and pulling until his hips pistoned in a demanding rhythm and he feared he would crush her as his desire blinded him to everything but their joining and ultimate goal. Her body stiffened under his and he felt the pulsing hot wash of her orgasm coat his cock. His body shuddered as he tried to control his own release, but he was unable to. They came together in a tangle of arms, legs, and frantic kisses.

His body pulsed, his seed emptying deep into her womb, and his heart thumped in time with hers. He bent his head and pressed his lips to the curve of her shoulder. Their heavy breathing echoed through the bedroom.

"I love you, Ruth Hallbrook," he whispered against her moist skin.

She rubbed her cheek against his hair. "I love you, too, my gentle giant," she murmured.

Her words seeped into his heart. He closed his eyes and tightened his arms around Ruth. He would never take for granted the magic of being able to hold her in his arms. Now that she was normal size again, he could show her the magic of his world.

CHAPTER FIFTEEN

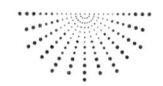

It was early afternoon by the time they emerged from the bedroom. Ruth felt like she was floating. Her body was both mellow and buzzing at the same time. It was also tingling in more than one place. Her nipples were super sensitive from all the loving they had received. It wasn't the only thing that was sensitive. Her thigh muscles, along with a few others, were reminding her that it had been a long, long time since they'd had this much of a workout.

A low moan and Koorgan's possessive hand on her ass let her know that she wasn't the only one regretting the fact that they finally had to get dressed and leave the sanctuary of his quarters. They wouldn't have left the room even then except for the fact that Koorgan had a meeting.

"Ruth! You're...," Gant stuttered, waving his hand up and down in shock.

Her lips twitched with amusement at Gant's open mouth. She couldn't resist walking up to him. Placing one slender finger under his chin, she pushed upward with a gentle pressure.

"You're catching flies, Gant," Ruth murmured with a soft laugh.

"You are... You are...," Gant kept repeating as he stared at her in confusion and wonder.

"You could say I had a sudden growth spurt last night. So, who are the idiots with a death wish that interrupted my awesome morning?" she inquired with a raised eyebrow as she nodded to the elegantly dressed delegation.

Gant frowned and looked over at where she had nodded. Koorgan was listening to one of the men with his arms folded across his chest. They were in the outer corridor near Koorgan's office. The man had immediately stopped Koorgan when he saw him.

"Pirates," Gant muttered with distaste.

Ruth frowned as she studied the six men. They all looked more than a little rough around the edges despite their finery. In fact, they looked like the sharks of Wall Street without the finely tailored high-priced suits.

The one talking with Koorgan was the least intimidating of the lot. The guy looked like he was a of couple years older than she was. He wore a white shirt, dark brown pants, boots, vest, and a black overcoat that hung almost to his knees.

Perfect for Halloween, she thought with amusement.

She took a moment to study the other men. They were each dressed in a similar style but their ensembles were in a variety of other colors that included feathered hats. One was even wearing a bright red coat. For a moment, Ruth wondered if they had raided her grandmother's attic before she died.

She returned her focus to the man talking to Koorgan. A flush of irritation rose in her cheeks when she saw that the man was now giving her an assessing look. She had dealt with enough assholes to know that he was gauging her reason to be there.

"Ruth, I would like you to look over these contracts, if you don't mind," Koorgan requested.

A satisfied smile twisted her lips when she saw the guy start with surprise at Koorgan's request. She gave Gant a wink when he sniggered under his breath and excused herself. She strode across the hallway to stand next to Koorgan, reached for the paperwork, and flashed a brief smile at the newcomers. The younger one frowned and raised an eyebrow when Koorgan wrapped his arm possessively around her waist.

"I'd be happy to, Koorgan. Do you mind if I take them into your office?" she replied.

"Not at all, my Lady," Koorgan replied before turning to look at the small group of men who had grown quiet. "Follow me."

Ruth stepped into the room when Koorgan politely held open the door for her. She walked over to one of the chairs situated next to the windows that overlooked the garden, turned, and sank down onto the plush upholstery. Within seconds, she was engrossed in the documents that Koorgan had handed her.

She glanced up when Koorgan held out a pen for her. With a grateful smile, she took the writing utensil from him, her lips parting in a soft hiss when he caressed her fingers before he released the pen. Her heated gaze followed him as he walked back to the group before she forced her mind to concentrate on the words in front of her and not on his ass. In the background, she could hear Koorgan and several of the men discussing the recent events that had happened on the Isle of Magic while two others stood off to the side.

~

Ashure Waves, better known as the King of the Pirates, stared at the woman sitting in the chair completely engrossed in the paperwork Koorgan had handed her. He had noticed her immediately when she walked down the corridor next to Koorgan. It would have been impossible to ignore her. She was different from the other women in the way she dressed, the way she walked, and the way she looked. She had the same mystique that Drago and Orion's mates had. He could tell that she was not from any of the Seven Kingdoms.

"Who is she?" the pirate Bleu LaBluff asked.

"I don't know, but I plan to find out. Keep Koorgan distracted," Ashure instructed.

LaBluff glanced at where the other four pirate captains were speaking with Koorgan, his eyes narrowing. He didn't look happy, but LaBluff would do as he was ordered. Ashure knew the last thing the other pirate captain wanted to do was irritate Koorgan on a personal level. Business dealings were one thing – messing with the man's woman was another.

"Be careful," LaBluff warned under his breath. "I saw the way Koorgan looked at her. He will be very protective of this one."

"Exactly. That makes her all the more valuable – and fun. It isn't often that I truly get to irritate the King of the Giants," Ashure replied with a smile.

"You have a death wish, Ashure," LaBluff muttered.

Ashure chuckled with amusement when LaBluff groaned. There might be six pirate captains in the room, but that didn't necessarily make the odds even when it came to a fight. Koorgan could probably whip five of them at once with one hand tied behind his back. The only one in the room that would have even half a chance of winning against Koorgan was Ashure, not that he wanted to test his theory. Ashure considered himself more of a lover than a fighter – though he never turned down a good fight when it presented itself.

"Someday your 'fun' is going to get us all killed," LaBluff commented under his breath.

"Nay, my friend. It is hard to lead a fleet of pirates if I have no pirates left to lead," he joked.

Ashure chuckled at LaBluff's string of muttered curses when the other pirate grudgingly turned and walked over to Koorgan. Drawn to the intriguing woman, Ashure turned and walked over to the chair next to Ruth and sank down.

He waited several seconds before he began to tap his fingers on the arm of the chair. He tapped louder when she still didn't acknowledge his presence. Shifting in his seat, he released an annoyed breath and crossed his legs when she continued to ignore him and kept reading instead.

"The bathrooms are down the corridor and to the left," she murmured without looking up from where she was making another notation on the contract.

"I don't need to use the facilities," Ashure responded with a raised eyebrow.

The woman tapped her bottom lip with the pen in her hand and marked on the contract again before she responded. Ashure's gaze followed the movement, exasperated that she wasn't paying him a bit of attention. Most females liked it when he expressed an interest in them. She finally pulled her focus away from the paperwork she was holding and looked across at him.

"Well, you could have fooled me with the way you are fidgeting in your seat," Ruth coolly stated.

Ashure's fingers froze and he studied Ruth with a mixture of surprise and disbelief for a moment before he laughed. This woman had an unusual sense of humor. If he didn't know better, he'd think she had just brushed him off.

His narrowed eyes took in every detail about her. Her hair was a dark, reddish-brown with streaks of blonde in it. It was short compared to the way the majority of females from the various isles wore theirs. She was also wearing long trousers and a white silk shirt similar to his, but hers was untucked and she wore a belt slung low around her full hips. It took a moment for him to realize that she was watching him with a slightly irritated expression.

"You do know that if you took a picture it would last longer, right? In case you missed it during your first drive-by gawking, I'm a little too busy right now to socialize," she added with a wave of her hand.

"So, when would you be available?" Ashure asked in a smooth, honeyed tone guaranteed to melt her resistance.

Ruth huffed a short laugh and shook her head. "I swear, it doesn't matter which world you're on, there are pricks in all of them. Let's see if I can make this clear enough for you. Go away. I'm not interested," she said in a low, very deliberate tone.

Ashure sat back, stunned at her dismissal. He raised his hand to rub his chin and grimaced. Perhaps he should have taken the time to clean up a bit better. The others had been anxious to meet with Koorgan and he had been tired and irritated by their whining.

"Perhaps I can change your mind later, when you are not so busy," Ashure said as he rose to his feet.

"Good luck with that," she muttered sarcastically.

Ashure stood in front of her for a moment, unsure of how to proceed. He had never encountered someone who was more interested in paperwork than in him. He pursed his lips, irritated at the dismissal, yet intrigued by it at the same time.

Someone this good with contracts would be an asset, he thought.

∼

Later that evening, Koorgan sat at the head of the dining table while Ashure sat to his left. Ruth sat to his right. Gant sat next to Ruth while Mike, Marina, and the other pirates were further down the table. Koorgan was trying to keep his attention on what Ashure was saying, but it was difficult. His focus kept turning to where Ruth was laughing at something Gant had said.

A sharp flare of jealousy flashed through him and then vanished when she turned to look at him. The expression in her eyes sent a shiver of need through him as he remembered their morning together. She must have been thinking the same thing because he felt her hand slide up his thigh.

"If I didn't know better, Koorgan, I'd think the mighty giant has fallen," Ashure dryly stated, lifting his wine glass to his lips.

Koorgan blinked several times when he realized that Ashure was speaking to him. A wave of irritation flashed through him. He didn't want to deal with the pirates at the moment; he wanted to concentrate on Ruth. He pursed his lips to keep from telling the man to take his unruly crew and depart from the Isle of the Giants. As much as he hated working with the bloody bastards, they helped to supply needed materials and relayed essential information that he wasn't likely to garner from the Ambassadors who came to talk trade.

"You know, I don't believe I have ever met anyone like her before," Ashure continued, his speculative glance running over Ruth.

"She is mine, Ashure. Do not doubt that," Koorgan warned.

Ashure turned and looked back at him with a disappointed expression. Koorgan wasn't fooled. Ashure would steal Ruth for a ransom or as an exotic prize to sell or trade if the opportunity presented itself.

"I feared you would say that. Which Kingdom is she from? I've been to all of them more than once except that of the Elementals, unfortunately. It is rather difficult to visit an Isle that doesn't touch the seas," Ashure replied.

"The Elemental King was determined to protect his people from Magna's dark powers," Koorgan responded with a shrug. "I would have done the same if it had been possible."

"The closure of the Isle of the Giants was a difficult decision, I'm sure. I appreciate that you allowed our continued trade negotiations. Perhaps, I can do business with Lady Ruth's people. I am always up for new clients," Ashure replied in a smooth tone.

Koorgan glared at the pirate king. "Ashure, do not take me for a fool. Ruth is off limits. I will tell you nothing about her or her people," Koorgan decreed in a steely tone.

Ashure narrowed his eyes in frustration and an uncharacteristic flash of anger briefly shone in his expression. Koorgan grimaced. He had suspected that Ruth rebuffing Ashure's attention would only increase the pirate's interest. While he appreciated her doing it, he was annoyed by the expected consequences. It was the nature of the beast to want what it could not have.

Ashure finally gave a forced laugh. "A pity. She is a fascinating woman, intelligent, exotic, and sharp tongued. Something tells me she would be just as interesting in a bed," he replied with a dismissive shrug.

Koorgan remained silent. He wasn't about to discuss his or Ruth's bedroom life with anyone, much less the Pirate King. He turned his attention to Ruth when she squeezed his thigh again.

"By the way," Ruth spoke up, "I meant to tell you that I've finished going over the contracts and have noted some suggestions. For pirates, they are amazingly honest in their trade negotiations – for the most part," Ruth said.

Ashure chuckled at Ruth's backhanded compliment. "We may be pirates, Lady Ruth, but we also have a code of honor – in our own way – when we conduct business with the different kingdoms. After all, it would be difficult to make a living if no one would negotiate with us," Ashure assured her with a slight incline of his head.

Ruth frowned. "And these kingdoms don't mind that you are robbing from their people and then selling their own stolen stuff back to them?" she questioned.

Ashure chuckled and shook his head. "Not at all, because we steal equally among the kingdoms – with the exception of the Isle of the Giants, that is, and never sell their own products back to them. That would be in bad taste, of course," he hastily added, glancing at Koorgan's stiff features.

"Of course," Ruth mockingly responded.

"So, I am curious. What brings you to the Isle of the Giants, Lady Ruth?" Ashure politely asked.

Ruth automatically glanced down the table where Mike was chatting with several of the other men. Koorgan reached under the table and squeezed her hand in warning. She returned his gesture to show that she understood.

"I had some unfinished business that I needed to resolve – much like you, I suspect. I heard that Koorgan was searching for an expert in economic, contract, and accounting matters. I happened to be in the right place at the right time to get the job," she explained.

"Oh, that's quite interesting. You were very fortunate, Koorgan, to have Lady Ruth suddenly appear like that," Ashure commented.

"You have no idea. It has been a long day. I'll have Gant escort you to the den for after-dinner drinks. There, you can go over the changes Ruth has made to the contracts. If you will excuse us, Ruth and I have a previous engagement that we must attend," Koorgan replied, pushing his chair back and standing up.

Ruth pushed her chair back as well and rose in unison with him. Their hands were still entwined. Ashure looked at him with a surprised expression before he hastily rose to his feet as well. He gave Koorgan a brief nod before he looked at Ruth. Koorgan was thankful the table was between Ashure and Ruth when he saw the mischievous glint in the other man's eyes.

"Until we meet again, Lady Ruth. I hope you – enjoy – your next engagement," Ashure said.

Ruth raised an eyebrow. "Oh, I fully intend to, Your Majesty," she replied.

"Ashure, please. The other sounds far too ostentatious," he lightly responded.

"Goodnight, Ashure," Ruth said.

"Goodnight, Lady Ruth," he murmured.

Koorgan could feel Ashure's eyes on them as they left. He looked back over his shoulder once and shot the Pirate King a look that warned him that he would not tolerate any misdeeds. Ashure bowed his head in acknowledgement of the warning. Whether the pirate actually abided by it was another story.

CHAPTER SIXTEEN

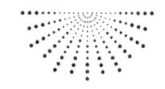

By the next morning, Koorgan decided he'd had enough of Ashure – for a long, long time. Especially when he saw the man chatting with Mike Hallbrook in the dining room. Ashure lifted his cup in salute, a pleased gleam in his unusual eyes.

Concerned that Ashure might be up to his usual tricks, he turned and crossed over to the table. He nodded to Mike, Marina, and Gant before he directed his attention to Ashure. Ashure sat back in his seat and looked around.

"Where is the lovely Lady Ruth? Exhausted from your – other commitments – last night?" Ashure inquired.

Koorgan ignored the taunt. "Gant will see to concluding the contracts today. I trust you and your men will be gone before dark," he said, his tone no longer welcoming.

"Of course," Ashure replied in a stiff voice. "As always, it was a pleasure doing business with you, Koorgan – and a pleasure meeting Lady Ruth. Please give her my sincere regrets at not being able to say goodbye."

"I won't," Koorgan replied.

He turned as Ruth stepped into the room. It was obvious from the expression on her face that she had heard his terse comment. He walked over to her and gently cupped her elbow, guiding her back out into the corridor.

"I was going to ask if everything was alright, but I don't think that is necessary. It's good to know I'm not the only one who can be a bit on the blunt side," she murmured.

"I want you to myself and I don't trust the bastard," Koorgan confessed with a grin.

Ruth chuckled. "Well, thank you for not telling Mike and Marina to get lost. I'd like to spend a little more time getting to know my new sister-in-law before you kick everyone off the Isle. I still can't believe that I'm going to be an aunt in a couple of months," she said with a grin, threading her arm through his.

"You'll get to see them later. At the moment, I'm feeling a little selfish and have other plans that I hope you will enjoy," he replied mischievously.

~

When Koorgan escorted her out through a narrow door, Ruth's breath caught at the beauty of the garden that lay hidden on the other side. She had discovered the small replica of the garden when she was exploring the dollhouse, but there was no comparison to the real one. Warmth swept through her when Koorgan looked down at her with so much heat in his gaze that she swore she could feel it scorch her.

She stopped and splayed her hands across his chest. "You know, if you keep looking at me like that, I'm going to have to do something about it," Ruth warned him with a knowing smile.

"Why do you think I brought you here? There are no windows along this section of the garden. The walls are high and covered with vines, and there are only two people who have a key to the door – myself and the head gardener who I gave the day off," he said.

She gasped when he suddenly swept her up into his arms. That wasn't an easy feat considering that she wasn't exactly slender. His eyes narrowed and a satisfied, wicked grin twisted his lips.

She wrapped her arm around his neck and glanced back and forth between where he was going and his face, afraid that she was too heavy for him to carry very far. A moment of insecurity washed through her before she pushed it away. She was who she was and she wasn't going to apologize to anyone for it.

"What is wrong?" he asked, seeing the fleeting emotion cross her face as they approached a vine covered gazebo.

She made a face. "I was just wishing I had lost those last twenty-five pounds I kept promising myself I would on my last birthday. Your poor back is probably about ready to break," she admitted with an apologetic look.

His laughter boomed in the deserted, enclosed garden, and Ruth was startled when he lifted her high enough to press a fierce kiss against her lips. She immediately responded, tightening her arms around his neck and deepening the kiss.

He finally broke their kiss and smiled down at her. "You are perfect the way you are. If you had lost any of that weight, I would have had to feed you more to put it back on. I like a woman I can hold on to, Ruth," he said.

This time it was her turn to pull his head down to give him a hot, open-mouthed, I-want-to-screw-your-brains-out kiss that told him he had said the right thing. They both groaned before he ripped his lips away from hers to search frantically around.

"We are alone. I was going to feed you before I ravished you, but I'm afraid you'll have to eat afterwards," he murmured.

"It's a good thing I'm only hungry for one thing then," she teased.

She trailed her fingers through the short strands of his hair on his neck, and shivered with need as he stepped into the gazebo and gently lowered her down onto the wide settee.

"I'll help you undress, then," she whispered, pulling him down over her. "After I do, I'll…" She leaned up and whispered what she planned to do in his ear.

"Goddess, you are a dangerous woman, Ruth," Koorgan muttered as he sat back just far enough to rip his shirt over his head.

∼

Ruth applied enough pressure on Koorgan's shoulders to let him know she wanted him to roll over onto his back. The move placed her on top of him. She straddled his waist and smiled down at him as she ran her hands up and down his bare chest. A hum of pleasure escaped her. He had a hairy chest. The soft, slightly curly hair felt good as she ran her fingers through it.

He gripped the bottom of her shirt and pulled it over her head, throwing it onto the chair next to the wide lounge chair. His fingers worked the clasp of her bra and it soon followed. She wiggled her way down his body, pressing hot, opened-mouthed kisses along the way.

Her fingers paused over his nipples. Koorgan's hips bucked underneath her when she tweaked them. He shot her a look of warning when she released a pleased chuckle at his reaction.

A soft moan of pleasure slipped from her when his hands cupped her breasts, playing with her taut nipples. She hated to pull away, but there were some sacrifices a woman had to make in order to give a guy a proper blow job, and at the moment, that was exactly what she wanted to do.

Her fingers gripped the fastenings of his trousers and she pulled them open. His hips rose when she gripped the sides and pulled them down. She slid off the end of the lounge, taking his trousers with her as she went. Then she pulled his shoes off and tossed them to the side.

He looked down his body at her. Ruth ran her hands up along her sides and cupped her breasts. The fire in his eyes flared and she tilted her head, wiggling her eyebrows at him. Sliding her hands back down, she quickly shed her pants and panties.

Bending down, she pressed a knee to the end of the lounge between his legs. She licked her lips as she slowly worked her way up. Her eyes were locked on his cock, which bobbed up and down with his anticipation.

"Will you quit torturing me, woman?" he groaned.

"Now where is the fun in making it quick and easy?" she retorted, rubbing her breasts against his right thigh.

"Just... remember... that what you give is what you'll get," he warned through gritted teeth.

She chuckled and nipped the inside of his leg. "But I'm enjoying torturing you so very... very... much," she murmured between kisses.

Koorgan's mock protest evaporated when she wrapped her hand around his cock and bent over him. His hips jerked and a partially smothered curse slipped from his lips. Ruth began a slow and purposeful assault on his senses, wrapping her lips around his bulbous head and sliding her mouth over him.

"Goddess, but I hope you never quit torturing me," he said.

Ruth hummed around him and he moaned again. She had never been wild about going down on a guy, but Koorgan had completely changed her mind. The power she felt at being able to give him pleasure was intoxicating. She could feel his body trembling as his fragile control melted a little more with each touch of her lips and tongue.

She didn't hold back. She used everything in her limited arsenal and a lot of her imagination to bring him to the peak. His hisses and moans proved that what she was doing was working.

"Enough, Ruth. Goddess, I can't hold back any longer," he declared in a barely recognizable voice.

He leaned up and gripped her under her arms, pulling her body up over his. Ruth was dripping with need and wasn't about to complain. She wrapped her hand around his engorged cock and straddled him.

Rising up, she aligned his cock and slowly impaled herself on his thick shaft. His hands tightened on her breasts as his hips rose. A shudder ran through her and she didn't try to hold back her cry of pleasure. Her hands wrapped around his wrists and she held his hands against her as she used her thigh muscles to ride him.

"Oh, yes! Damn, Koorgan, this feels so good," she moaned.

She leaned forward against his hands and gripped his shoulders as she began riding him harder and faster. The movement exerted the perfect pressure on her clit. She could feel her orgasm building.

Her breathing grew faster, more erratic as the pressure built inside her. Her head bowed and she closed her eyes, visualizing the movement of his cock inside her. That image had no sooner formed in her mind than he pinched her nipples, sending her over the edge.

Her eyes opened and her head lifted just far enough that she could stare into his eyes with dazed, wild eyes as her body shook from the intensity of her release. He drove his cock deep into her and released a primitive, guttural shout as he came with her.

Her body gripped his, refusing to release him. She could feel his cock swell, stretching her as he came, and she trembled with pleasure.

Koorgan's hands slid across her skin and then he drew her down to lay on top of him, lifting one leg enough to wrap over her. Deep inside her, Ruth could still feel his cock throbbing and her feminine depths pulsing in response.

"I think you've melted my bones," she whispered, her cheek pressed again his chest.

Koorgan chuckled and pressed a kiss to the top of her head. "I was thinking the same thing. It is a good thing you are on top," he teased.

"You totally rock as a lover, Koorgan," she murmured in a drowsy voice. "I think my mind is shattered. I'm going to need a lot of super glue to put it back together."

"I'll only shatter it again the next time we make love," he replied, rubbing his cheek against her hair.

Ruth wanted to reply, but she honestly didn't have the strength at the moment – or the mental capacity – to process anything else. They had spent most of the night making love, only to fall asleep just before sunrise. Her body had never felt so relaxed or content.

Sleep pulled her into its embrace. She hoped Koorgan didn't plan on going anywhere for a while. She was limper than a wet noodle. A smile curved her lips when his arms tightened around her and he released a deep, satisfied sigh.

This is so much better than being a Lilliputian. Giants have all the fun, she thought with a deep, happy sigh.

∽

Koorgan stirred on the wide settee, his arm still wrapped around Ruth. He reached over to the chair and pulled his discarded shirt off of it. Trying not to wake her, he tenderly covered her.

Another deep sigh of contentment slipped from him. His original plan for bringing her here this morning had been to ask her to be his wife. He knew that she was the one destined to be by his side.

He still intended to ask her – just not in the order that he had planned. His first thought had been to feed her breakfast, get down on one knee afterwards and ask for her hand in marriage, then ravish her. It looked like they were going to be doing things backwards – not that he was complaining.

His fingers rose to caress her face. She had fallen asleep shortly after their heated joining. A frown creased his brow when he saw a faint glow rise up from her skin as he ran his finger along her cheek.

His heart pounded with alarm when he saw the glow spreading across the rest of her body, and he panicked as he realized what was happening. With trembling fingers, he shook her.

"Ruth – Ruth, wake up. Oh, my heart, no – please, no. Ruth!" he choked out as a sense of helplessness engulfed him.

Ruth's eyelashes fluttered for a moment before she looked up at him. Then her eyes widened as he began to grow in front of her eyes and she clutched him tightly while she still could, her expression of fear and panic swiftly changing to unbearable sorrow. Cupping her cheek, Koorgan tried to hold onto her, but he could see the magic swirling around her.

"Koorgan," she whispered in despair. "No! Please... No!" she begged hoarsely as she raised her hand to touch his cheek.

Within seconds, Koorgan's hands cupped Ruth's body as she lay weeping uncontrollably. He turned and sat on the edge of the settee, holding her tenderly in front of him. His heart wrenched at the grief in her sobs. He was barely able to contain his own tears, afraid that if he started, he would drown her with them.

CHAPTER SEVENTEEN

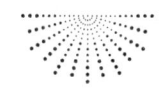

"Hush, my Ruth, the magic worked once. It will surely work again," he murmured, trying to console himself as well as her.

Ruth twisted and sat up in his hand, glaring up at him in frustration. She angrily wiped at the dampness on her cheeks and pushed her hair back from her face, emitting a loud sniff. A stubborn expression settled over her features as she stood up and wrapped her arms around her bare waist.

"This is really pissing me off!" she retorted, stomping her foot. "What kind of crazy magic gives me what I wished for, then takes it away? That is totally fuc – ucked up," she added, hiccupping and wiping her face again.

Koorgan's lips twitched at her mutinous expression. He knew the situation wasn't funny, but damn if Ruth didn't look adorable stomping her tiny foot in his hand and giving him that cross look like she was about to whip someone's ass. He raised his hand up so he could look into her eyes.

"I will not stop until I find a way to restore you to your true size, Ruth. I swear. What did you do before?" he asked.

Ruth bit her lip. "There was a shell in my bed, like the one Magna gave me, except in miniature. I'm pretty sure it is the same one, I just happened to find it after misplacing it, but it said something different this time, just a single word. I made a wish and repeated the word that I heard, but nothing happened – at least not at first," she replied with a frown. "I need to get back to the dollhouse."

Koorgan nodded and lowered her to the cushion. He rose to his feet and quickly gathered his clothes and dressed before picking up Ruth's discarded garments. He turned and placed his hand down next to the pillow so she could climb back onto his hand.

"I need clothes. I didn't realize how cold it was out here without your arms around me," she grumbled with a pout.

"Here," Koorgan replied, lifting her to his breast pocket. "You can snuggle close to my heart."

Ruth rolled her eyes, pulling a chuckle from Koorgan as she slid down into his pocket and settled herself. He glanced down at her. His eyes heated as memories of how he had just touched her naked form washed through him.

"You can keep that look to yourself, Koorgan," Ruth said, snuggling closer to his warmth. "It's not going to get you anything until we figure out this mess."

"We will, Ruth. I've had a taste of you, my beauty. I won't settle for anything less than a full life together," Koorgan vowed.

Ruth bowed her head, but not before he saw the fear and doubt in her expression. Folding her clothes, he stepped out of the gazebo and strode back through the gardens toward the palace. He would contact the Director of Archives again, and this time, the man better have some answers for him.

∽

Several hours later, Ruth lay on her bed in the dollhouse. She turned the shell in her hand over and over. No matter how many times she made a wish, nothing happened. No mattered how many times she placed it to her ear, she heard nothing; not a whisper, not the sound of the waves, just silence

A single tear coursed down her cheek. Clutching the shell in her hand, she rose off the bed and placed the shell into the tiny box on the table.

Koorgan had left her to go down the hall to the library. He had invited her, but she had refused, hoping that the magic in the shell would work if he wasn't there to see it.

"Stupid, defective magical shell," Ruth groaned in frustration. "Give a girl a taste of heaven, then take it away. I can't believe Magna would do that, not after everything that happened to her."

Ruth turned when she heard the sound of the door opening. A frown creased her brow and she hurriedly stepped out onto the terrace.

"Koorgan, did you…?" Ruth's voice died when a man stepped out of the shadows.

This wasn't Koorgan. This was one of the pirates from yesterday. Fear coursed through Ruth when she saw his avaricious glance turn toward her. Cursing silently, she wished she had kept her mouth shut.

"Well, well, well," LaBluff said with a chuckle as he walked toward her. "I knew Ashure wanted you, but I bet even he didn't realize just how valuable you would be. It appears the King of the Giants has a not so giant-size treasure."

Ruth sneered at the man when he bent closer to look at her. She edged back toward the doorway to her room.

"I'm not going to state the obvious that you aren't supposed to be here. The only reason you would be is to steal something from Koorgan, and I really shouldn't have to point out what a really dumbass idea that is. He'll smash you to smithereens," she snapped, taking several small steps backwards.

"Yes, I imagine he would, if he knew," LaBluff stated as he reached out, snapped the door to the bedroom closed, and stuck a small, decorative stick pin into wood in front of the door to prevent her from escaping into the castle. "I don't think so, my tiny treasure. I might just keep you for myself."

Ruth turned and tugged on the door but LaBluff scooped her up. Opening her mouth, Ruth let out a piercing scream. At least it sounded piercing to her. LaBluff closed his hands over her and shook her.

Her screamed turned into a muffled cry of terror. She covered her head when he began to squeeze her between his hands. It wouldn't take much for him to crush her. She felt herself roll when he turned his hands over and eased them apart far enough to peer inside.

"I think you understand the warning, my Lady. If you so much as make a squeak, I'll start breaking bones," he threatened.

A shudder ran through Ruth before she could hide it. "Why don't you go pick on someone your own size! When I'm big again, I'm going to shove your balls up your ass," she snapped.

"That sounds like a very painful thing to endure. Keep your threats to yourself, my Lady. You will bring me riches and maybe – just maybe – Koorgan can buy you back," LaBluff chuckled.

Ruth fought her growing sense of panic when he carried her over to the golden bird cage that had been her original home. He reached in, lowering his hand until she rolled out of it onto the floor. He shut and locked the door to the cage before draping the sheer, dark blue lace cover over it.

She stood up and looked through the bars. Ruth could make out that the pirate was heading for the balcony door. He peered through the clear glass before he opened it and stepped out.

"Now, unless you want me to toss your crushed remains to the birds, I suggest that you stay quiet," he quietly instructed.

"You'll be begging for hemorrhoids by the time I get done with you," Ruth hissed as she held onto the thin bars of the bird cage to keep from being thrown around. "Koorgan is going to rip you apart, limb by thieving limb."

"Not before I crush you if you aren't silent," LaBluff threatened, shaking the cage once again.

Ruth smothered a cry when she was propelled off the floor of her golden prison, weightless for a moment. She clamped her lips tightly together. The last thing she needed to do was lose her head and act like a defenseless ninny. She was smart. She and Mike used to get into all kinds of scrapes when they were kids. Hell, she had been in a few as an adult – now being a perfect example. She just needed to focus on finding a way out.

Wrapping her arm around one of the bars, she glanced around the cage. Her eyes narrowed on the two sliding parts that were used to insert food and water for the birds. They were a little high, but she would figure out a way to get up there. She could accomplish almost anything once she set her mind to it.

"I'll get out of here, and when I do, I'm going to kick LaBluff's ass," she muttered, holding on as the cage swung crazily again.

CHAPTER EIGHTEEN

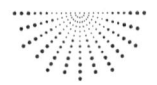

Koorgan drained his glass again and placed it on the bar. His hands curled around the glass before he turned and hurled crystal goblet into the fireplace. The sound of shattering glass reverberated through the room. Koorgan turned and gripped the edge of the bar, bending forward as pain, grief, and an overwhelming sense of helplessness coursed through his body.

He closed his eyes when Gant placed his untouched drink down next to him and reached out to grip his shoulder. Taking in a shuddering breath, he straightened and turned to look at his friend with tortured eyes. Gant returned his look with one of deep concern.

"What happened?" Gant quietly asked.

"The magic – it didn't last. I held her and watched as she shrank before my eyes. I have never felt so helpless in all of my life, Gant. Her tortured sobs – I have held the greatest gift any man could wish for within my arms and I could do nothing to stop the magic from…," Koorgan's throat tightened and he couldn't go on.

Gant frowned. "What do you need me to do?" he asked, his tone determined.

Koorgan's expression turned steely. He reached out and gripped Gant's shoulder.

"I want you, Mike, and Marina – if she is able to go without harm to herself and Mike's babe – to return to Ruth's world and bring back Magna. I don't care how you do it, bring me the Sea Witch. It was her magic that brought Ruth here and changed her. She will help me or I will personally squeeze the life out of her," Koorgan ordered.

Gant gave him a brief nod and pulled away. "Consider it done," he grimly replied.

"Gant," Koorgan called in a serious tone as Gant turned and headed for the door.

Gant paused and looked back. "Yes?"

"Take care. The Sea Witch is very powerful," Koorgan cautioned.

Gant grinned. "You know better than anyone that giants have their own brand of magic. I will not fail you or the Kingdom, my King," he vowed.

"Thank you, my friend," Koorgan quietly replied.

Gant bowed his head once more before he pulled open the door and exited. Koorgan picked up Gant's untouched glass of brandy and drained it before he set it back on the bar. He had no doubt that Mike and Marina would assist Gant. Mike would do anything necessary to help his sister.

Koorgan glanced out the window. In the distance, he could see four of the six pirate ships leaving port. Only Ashure's and one other remained.

One less thing to worry about, he thought with relief.

He had no doubt that if Ashure knew about Ruth's current condition, the situation could have become much more complicated. Everyone knew that the King of the Pirates loved to steal the most unusual treasures he could find and keep them for himself.

"This is it, King Koorgan," the elderly director called out in a voice that trembled with age. He pointed to a picture in one of the old books he had pulled from the shelf. "This is what you are looking for. The mythical mushrooms said to be the first ones of their kind – those planted by the Goddess herself."

Koorgan turned and stepped closer to the table. He stared down at the beautiful illustration on the page. Bordered in gold, the picture showed a place deep within the forest. Moonlight shone down through the massive trees onto the ground in a small clearing. In the center of the clearing was a group of mushrooms unlike any that he had ever seen before.

Amidst the mushrooms were the moving images of Koorgan's ancestors. They looked no taller than Ruth. One of the figures wore an emblem of the crown upon his chest. He dismounted from his steed and walked slowly toward the mushroom. Raising his sword, he cut off pieces of the mushroom and handed them to those standing behind him.

In the third image, he could see a small group of men and women eating pieces of the freshly cut mushrooms. As they did, the figures began to grow. The giants knelt beside the plant and carefully dug it up.

Koorgan's gaze shifted to the old man standing silently beside him. Swallowing, he pointed to the picture. This was what Ruth needed.

"Where is it?" Koorgan demanded.

"Alas, all records of the plant were destroyed," the Director of the Archives muttered, reaching over to turn the page. "You can see the next page has been removed. The only ones who can remove an enchanted page are a member of the royal house or…"

"The witch who enchanted the books in the first place," Koorgan replied under his breath. "Where is the Spellbinder?"

"She lives deep within the woods, King Koorgan," the old man replied. "No one knows for sure where."

Koorgan turned back the page and stared at the images again. There was something vaguely familiar about the image. His eyes narrowed on a small stone structure. It looked like the wall of a…

Lifting his head, he stared blindly down the corridor. He thought he might know where the Spellbinder lived. He had been there a little over a month ago.

"Say nothing to anyone about this," Koorgan ordered, turning on his heel.

"Yes, my King," the old man replied, watching as Koorgan strode away.

Koorgan hurried back down the winding corridors to his rooms. He would take Ruth with him. If all went well, they would be together, forever, hopefully before the end of the day. Pushing open the door to his living quarters, he called out, "Ruth! Ruth, I believe I know a way to…," he shouted as he rushed through the room. He paused in the doorway to their bedroom, stiffening when he saw the decorative pin stuck in the door leading from the terrace to the master bedroom. "Ruth!" he whispered.

* * *

Gant entered the dining room. His attention focused on where Mike and Marina were talking. They both looked up at him and smiled when he walked toward them.

"Morning, Gant. Have you seen…? What's wrong?" Mike demanded.

Gant knew his face conveyed his concern. He pulled out the chair across from the couple and sat down. He lifted his hand and waved the servant away.

"Ruth has shrunk again. Koorgan has ordered me to journey to your world and bring Magna back," he said, cutting straight to the heart of the matter.

Marina gasped and shook her head. "Does he have any idea how dangerous that would be? Not only to return to Mike's world, but to try to capture a witch as powerful as Magna?" she said in a low, dismayed voice.

Gant shrugged. "The danger matters not to me. Returning with Magna and getting her to help Ruth is all that matters," he said.

"Isn't there is another way? I mean, Ruth was normal yesterday and this morning. Surely that means whatever magic that caused her to shrink is wearing off," Mike reasoned.

Gant shook his head. "Time is running out," he murmured.

"What do you mean 'Time is running out?' Running out for whom? Ruth?" Mike asked with concern.

Gant looked at Marina before he focused on Mike. "Nay – for the giants. Koorgan must marry within the next five days. He has chosen Ruth," he reluctantly shared.

"Excuse me? Why the rush?" Mike asked, confused.

"It is the magic," Marina answered, covering Mike's hand with her own.

Gant gave a brief nod. "Yes, it is the magic. Each Kingdom is ruled by a special magic. The magic of the giants hinges on the King of the Giants marrying someone not from our Kingdom – someone who brings balance and unity to our people," he explained.

"What happens if he doesn't marry in less than a week? Is he even sure that Ruth wants to marry him? Don't get me wrong, I'm not opposed to Koorgan or anything, but Ruth isn't likely just to fall in line with Koorgan's sudden desire to marry her. She had a bad experience once before and hasn't exactly been overly eager to jump back into dating, much less matrimony," Mike said.

Gant's face tightened. "If Koorgan does not marry, the giants will not be giants anymore, and it is obvious that she cares deeply for him. Regardless, I have my orders. I will do anything to save my Kingdom, Mike. I ask that you help, if not for us, then for the sake of your sister," he quietly stated.

Mike looked at Marina who nodded. "You have seen for yourself how powerful the magic of our world is, but if one Kingdom is lost, all Kingdoms will be lost as well. This is not just about the Isle of the Giants, it is about all the isles of the Seven Kingdoms," she softly added.

"What about our daughter? Will using your magic or traveling to my world endanger either of you?" Mike quietly asked, reaching out to caress her protruding abdomen.

Marina shook her head. "No, neither will harm LaDonna. She is strong – and safe," she replied, placing her hand over his.

"If anything goes wrong, you protect yourself and our daughter, do you understand? That is your first priority," Mike instructed with a deep sigh.

"I will. I promise," she said, squeezing his hand in reassurance.

"Can you open a portal?" he asked.

Marina's eyes twinkled with determination. "Yes. I might have memorized the spell Queen Magika cast – just in case," she replied with a small, satisfied smile.

Mike leaned to the side and brushed a kiss across Marina's lips. "I love you," he murmured before turning to look at Gant. "When do we leave?"

"Gather whatever you want to take with you. I'll meet you in the lower garden in fifteen minutes," Gant instructed.

"We will be ready," Marina replied, sliding her chair back and standing up.

Koorgan looked up from where he was kneeling on the grounds below his bedroom balcony. A set of boot prints in the soft soil formed tracks that led away from the palace. Rage washed across his face as he stood. He looked at the five guards standing at attention.

"Shut down the docks. No one is permitted to leave the Isle of the Giants. I want every pirate ship there searched. Hunt down the ones that have already left and bring them back – and find the Pirate King and bring him to my office," he ordered in a harsh voice.

"Yes, your Majesty. I will personally oversee the search of each ship," Edmond, his third-in-command, stated, then turned to do just that, taking the guards with him.

Koorgan stood looking out toward the harbor. If necessary, he would string up all the pirates until someone told him where Ruth was located. Guilt swept through him that he had failed to protect her.

"I will find you, my love," he vowed, clenching his fists.

CHAPTER NINETEEN

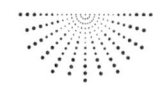

Three hours earlier:

Ruth clung to the bars of the golden cage. It was hard to do anything else with the way that doofus LaBluff was swinging the damn thing. If he would just put the cage down or walk a little less erratically, she could enact the plan she had been putting together in her head.

One thing she knew for certain, she needed to escape *before* the nasty cretin made it back to his ship. On a positive note, LaBluff, in his desire to appear casual and non-threatening, had taken the scenic way back to the docks. Perhaps he was afraid she would cause some kind of commotion if he went through the village to the port.

"Damn," he muttered, drawing her attention.

Through the sheer blue haze of the fabric, she saw LaBluff looking around. It took a moment for her to realize why he was a little antsy. The jerk needed to pee and from the way he was doing the jig – pretty badly.

LaBluff set the cage down next to a rock while he hurried over to water a tree along the path. Ruth released her grip on the bars and scrambled over to the sponge that had been her first bed. The soft, pliable material had tilted up on end during the journey and a corner of it had become lodged between two of the golden bars that framed the cage.

Ruth used the holes in the sponge as a ladder and climbed up to the opening meant to facilitate sliding in the food and water trays. She pushed and wiggled the latch on one of the doors until it popped open. Sliding her leg over the opening, she twisted until she was hanging from her waist out of the cage. She felt behind her with one hand.

If I can... just... reach... the blue... fabric, she thought.

She almost had a hand on it when LaBluff returned and picked up the cage. The jarring movement toppled her over the edge and she slid down the thin bars of the bird cage. She dangled from the bottom of the frame for a second before a bump against his leg loosened her hold and sent her tumbling downward. Ruth bit back her terrified scream and braced for her impact with the ground.

A hiss of surprise slipped from her when she landed in the soft center of a flower. Her hands desperately reached for the filament as the bright yellow bloom slowly tipped over with her added weight. She slid out of the flower and into the grass with a cushioned thump and a cloud of dislodged yellow-orange pollen. She was covered in the stuff.

Turning, she looked up in shock at her good fortune. The flower had broken what could have been a very nasty fall. Standing up, she watched with a mixture of relief and satisfaction as LaBluff continued on his merry way, oblivious to the fact that she was no longer his prisoner.

"Sucker!" she sneered before turning to look at the forest with a sigh.

It's going to be a long, long journey back to the palace, she thought with dismay.

∼

Present Time:

Koorgan paced back and forth in front of Ashure and a very battered LaBluff. His fists clenched as he turned on his heel to stare at the two men. LaBluff was touching his bruised jaw with a wary expression. If he did not find out what he needed to know from these two, he would hunt down Ashure's entire fleet.

"Where is she?" Koorgan demanded.

Ashure straightened the cuffs of his shirt and shrugged. "I told you, I have no idea what you are talking about. I have not had the pleasure of seeing the lovely Lady Ruth since this morning in the dining room," the King of the Pirates stated. "LaBluff, what about you?"

"I don't know what you are talking about either," LaBluff said.

Koorgan snapped his fingers. Edmond approached carrying the golden cage. The contents were missing and a torn piece of sheer blue fabric hung from the outside of it. Ashure frowned in confusion when he saw the cage while LaBluff looked away.

"That is a nice bird cage, Koorgan. Am I supposed to know its significance?" Ashure questioned with a raised eyebrow.

"Are you saying you have never seen this before?" Koorgan demanded.

Ashure studied the cage. "I'm really not into birds. The gold is nice – if it is real. Let me guess, you named a bird after your sweetheart and think that either LaBluff or I took the bird. I would have taken the cage and left the creature, honestly. Birds are noisy, messy creatures that have disgustingly wet poo," he retorted with a shudder.

Koorgan stepped forward until he towered over Ashure. "I'm not talking about birds, Ashure. I'm talking about Ruth!" He turned to LaBluff. "What about you? You seem to be far more uncomfortable than your king. What have you done with the future Queen of the Giants?" he growled.

LaBluff scowled and Ashure shook his head. "As I've already stated, we've done nothing with your woman, Koorgan. I am still trying to understand what the cage has to do with your betrothed," he reiterated.

Koorgan's sharp glare narrowed on Ashure. Rage poured through him when the male shrugged his shoulders, and appeared convincingly baffled. Stepping forward, Koorgan wrapped one hand around the pirate king's throat and lifted him off the floor.

"I warned you, Ashure. If anything happens to Ruth, I will hunt down every pirate and hang you from the cliffs," Koorgan hissed, squeezing. "Ruth! She is six inches high. She was in my private quarters and either you or one of your kind took her. No one else was leaving just as she disappeared. No one other than her family and my people even knew she was here, except the six of you *pirates*!"

Ashure raised his hands in surrender, and spoke disturbingly normally, as if there was currently no pressure against his throat at all. "Alright, alright, I can look into it. It wasn't me, I can assure you, but as you say, we are pirates. If it was one of mine, I will handle the matter. Your lady will be returned if at all possible, you have my word."

"Make it possible. This was found holding the door to her room," Koorgan gritted out, pulling the decorative pin from his pocket and holding it up. "Do you recognize it?"

Ashure looked at the pin, then his scrutiny moved to LaBluff. Koorgan seized on the information Ashure had conveyed with that look. He released Ashure and stepped back, turning his attention on LaBluff.

LaBluff shot an alarmed look at Ashure and staggered back several steps. "Now wait one minute. Ashure said he was the one who wanted the woman."

Koorgan took one look at LaBluff's panicked expression and quietly said, "But you were the one who took her."

"I – Ashure…," LaBluff stammered.

Edmond and another guard lunged to grab the pirate. LaBluff struck Edmond in the face with his elbow and pulled a knife from the sheath of the other guard, darting forward with the knife before freezing unnaturally in mid-strike as Ashure stepped in front of Koorgan. LaBluff's eyes were panicked as he fought to break the magical hold Ashure had over him, but he was defenseless against such dark magic. Ashure disarmed his second-in-command, and returned the knife to the guard.

Koorgan had never seen the Pirate King like this. Ashure's silver eyes swirled with color and a black mist rose around him. Koorgan knew at that moment why Nali had insisted that the alien creature who had taken over Magna must never get near Ashure.

"Tell me the truth," Ashure commanded.

Beads of sweat dampened LaBluff's skin. As the seconds ticked by, blood began to drip from his nose. LaBluff's lips moved and words poured out of his mouth.

"I took her. I was going to kill the woman and make it look like you had done it. When I entered the room, I saw… she had shrunk. I decided to take her instead. I thought not only could I… still frame you with her disappearance, but… but… sell her as well," LaBluff choked out.

"Why would you betray me, LaBluff?" Ashure murmured in a deceptively calm tone.

The sweat beading on LaBluff's brow had changed to droplets of blood. Blood also began to slide down his cheeks from the corners of his eyes.

"To rule… I wanted to rule. You… give away too much," LaBluff finally whispered.

Ashure's lips curved into a sardonic smile and he shook his head. Koorgan started to take a step forward, but stopped when Ashure raised his hand – palm outward – and stopped him. The Pirate King kept his intense focus on LaBluff.

"Where is the woman?" Ashure asked in an almost hushed voice.

"I don't know," LaBluff replied.

"Where is the woman?" Ashure repeated in a louder, harsher tone.

LaBluff's tortured scream filled the room. The pirate's body stiffened and jerked. The black mist enveloping Ashure spread out and began surrounding LaBluff.

"I don't know! She… she escaped. I stopped… Please, no… Goddess, no!! What are you? Oh, Goddess, no…!" LaBluff's agonized scream sent a shiver through Koorgan.

The mist slowly engulfed LaBluff's body. The man's flesh melted until nothing but a bleached skeleton remained. Even that did not last long. As the mist returned to Ashure, the bones turned to dust, and LaBluff's clothing fell to the floor.

Ashure stood frozen for several long seconds until the mist had completely disappeared – only then did he lower his still raised arm to his side and turn his head to look at Koorgan. Typical of Ashure, the Pirate King straightened the cuffs of his sleeves before he gave Koorgan a cordial smile.

"LaBluff stopped to urinate on a tree along the road that led to a cove not far from the harbor. I suspect that is where Ruth escaped," he calmly stated.

Koorgan placed his hand on Edmond's arm, lowering the pistol the guard had aimed at Ashure. He had no desire to give Ashure time to use his dark magic on him, but he also needed more information.

"Give me one good reason why I should not kill you now, Ashure," Koorgan quietly demanded.

Ashure's expression was resigned as he looked into Koorgan's cold eyes. "Because I can help you find Lady Ruth," he softly replied.

Koorgan debated whether he needed help from a person like Ashure when – if the pirate could be believed – he already knew the general area Ruth had last been seen, but the faster he found her, the more likely she would be unharmed. He nodded. With a wave of his hand, the guards around Ashure lowered their weapons. He flexed his fingers, resisting the urge to test whether whatever magic Ashure had used on LaBluff would work on him.

"How can you help?" Koorgan demanded.

Ashure's lips pursed for a moment before he relaxed again. "I have a magic mirror. It can show me where the woman is," he reluctantly admitted.

"Where is it?" he commanded.

A flash of irritation swept through Ashure's eyes. "In the top drawer of my desk in my cabin. You'll need my keys to enter both the room and the desk – unless you'd like to see your men in the same condition as LaBluff," he added with a wry smile.

"Give me the keys," Koorgan ordered.

He kept a wary gaze on Ashure as the pirate pulled a ring of keys from the inside of his pocket. He glanced at Edmond and motioned for the guard to take the keys.

"I want these back," Ashure warned before he dropped them into the guard's hand.

"Bring this magic mirror to me," Koorgan ordered Edmond. "I want everything stripped off their ships."

"Right away, your Majesty," Edmond replied.

Koorgan nodded and continued speaking to Ashure. "If you are indeed helping me, Ashure, I thank you, but even so, if Ruth isn't returned to me safely, I'll still hang every last one of you from the northern cliffs," he threatened.

Ashure grimaced. "Isn't this a little harsh, Koorgan? I've dealt with the thief – though I have to admit I'm a little perturbed that he was trying to frame me, so I would have killed him anyway once I found out. Still, the thief is dealt with," he reasoned with a wave of his hands.

"You are lucky I believe that you knew nothing of Ruth's disappearance or you would be wishing for your own death to come as quickly as LaBluff's did," Koorgan warned.

"I… see. Well… surely if Ruth is found, you can be a little more reasonable. We have had a long profitable relationship after all and I am trying to help," Ashure stressed in a cordial tone.

Koorgan took a step toward Ashure and paused, not breaking the staring contest between them. Seconds ticked by before he responded, "If she is found, I will return you to your empty ships and ban you from ever setting foot on the Isle of the Giants again."

Ashure's eyes bored into Koorgan's before he released a loud sigh. "Fair enough – I guess. I still think we should be allowed to keep what we've purchased – and make the 'forever' portion of this deal more like a month – or two," he hastily added.

"Lock him up until I return," Koorgan ordered.

Ashure rolled his eyes. "Really? You have my ship, where could I possibly go? I hope you have a clearer head when you get back. Lady Ruth will tell you I had nothing to do with her abduction," he yelled.

Koorgan ignored Ashure's protests. His mind was on Ruth and all of the horrible things that could happen to her. He hurried down the steps, yelling for the stable boy to bring Genisus to him. Minutes later, he was galloping through the gate, heading for the port.

CHAPTER TWENTY

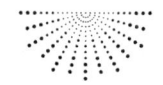

Yachats, Oregon

Mike eased the SUV up Gabe Lightcloud's long narrow driveway. Marina's portal had brought them to his own house. His SUV had been in the garage and Ruth's car had been returned out front. At least he wouldn't have to add grand theft to the kidnapping charge he was about to commit.

"Are you okay back there, Gant?" Mike asked.

"Yes. This – machine – is interesting," Gant muttered.

"He hates it," Marina chuckled.

"Yes," Mike agreed.

"Why could you not just open the portal here?" Gant complained.

Marina half turned in her seat. "I was familiar with Mike's house, so I could open a portal there. It helps if you know where you are going. Also, magic can leave a trace in the air. Magna is a very powerful witch. She would have felt the wave of magic since it is not common here," she explained.

Mike glanced in the rearview mirror. "Are you sure this will work?" he asked Gant, pulling to the side of the driveway.

"Yes. The combined use of the sleeping powder and Marina's magic will put Magna to sleep long enough for Marina to open another portal to our world – in theory," Gant replied.

Mike twisted and scowled at Gant. "What do you mean 'in theory'? I knew I should have left Marina home. There had to be another way," he growled.

"I've never exactly used this before," Gant confessed.

"That's it. You two stay here," Mike snapped, pushing open the door.

"Mike," Marina began, pushing open her door and sliding out.

"How do you open this thing?" Gant called out, pushing all the buttons and panels he could see on the door.

"I suggest all of you put your hands in the air," a deep voice interjected.

Mike twisted and slowly raised his hands when Gabe Lightcloud stepped out with a shotgun firmly pressed against his broad shoulder. Mike's expression darkened when Gabe motioned for Marina to step around the car, and he backed up enough to slowly open the car door for Gant.

"Put the weapon down," Mike ordered.

Gabe shook his head. "If I remember right, you disappeared and aren't with the police force at the moment. No one will know if I put a bullet in your head," he replied.

"No!" Marina hissed with alarm and lifted her hands.

The shotgun shattered, each piece flying in a different direction. Gabe cursed loudly, and Mike reached for the gun at his waist. He had barely pulled it from his holster when it vanished out of his hand.

He scanned the area for Magna, and Gant turned in her direction at the same time Mike did. Magna was standing next to Kane Field. Her hair floated around her and her brilliant green eyes glowed with the magic flowing through her.

Gant threw the enchanted bag of sleeping dust at Magna. The small bag flew through the air, propelled at top speeds by the spell Marina had placed on it. A split second before it connected with the Sea Witch, Kane lunged in front of her. The pouch struck him in the center of his back and exploded, covering him in dust that sparkled for a moment before disappearing.

Mike watched Kane stiffen and then fall. He would have landed hard if not for Magna's arms sweeping up around him to lower him gently to the asphalt driveway. Her distressed cry pierced Mike with guilt, but he didn't have time to dwell on it. Gabe was rounding the car to attack Gant.

The two men's arms locked around each other. For a split second, the odds looked pretty even – then Gant began to grow, which caused Magna to look up, Kane unconscious on the ground by her side, her focus now on Gabe and Gant. The situation was quickly escalating out of control.

"Gant, stand down!" Mike shouted. "Marina, help Kane. Gabe, let him go."

"I don't fucking have him," Gabe snapped, struggling to break free of the massive hand that was wrapped around his body.

"Why are you doing this? Why? I have tried to correct the damage I was compelled to do. Why can't I live in peace?" Magna yelled, her skin beginning to glow brighter as she knelt beside Kane while keeping her stare focused on Gabe.

"Magna, the spell on him is cast by a giant's magic. You can't reverse it without endangering him," Marina warned when she saw Magna's hand slide over Kane and sensed her power building.

Magna's glare shifted to Gant. Mike swallowed. He'd seen the giants at their full size before. Gant had stopped growing at about twenty feet. That was all he needed to hold Gabe as if he were a doll.

"Gant, release him," Mike instructed.

"Not until you and Marina have returned to the Isle of the Giants with Magna. If she refuses to go, I'll crush him," Gant threatened.

"No!" Magna swiftly rose to her feet.

Marina intercepted her and raised her hands, her eyes glittering with warning. Mike felt like groaning. So much for a discreet abduction and disappearance – and keeping Marina and their child safe!

"Stop," Mike said in a low, calm tone. "We already have the leverage we need now that Magna wants the spell on her man reversed."

Gant's gaze swung down to him, and the giant unintentionally squeezed his hand in frustration. Gabe groaned from within Gant's hand, and Magna softly cried out in denial.

"I will go with you – just please – please, let him go. I promise, I will go with you and you can do whatever you want. Don't hurt him anymore," Magna pleaded, dropping her hands to her side.

"No!" Gabe snapped. "Fuck, no, Magna. Fight, damn it. You fight them!"

She took a step forward and shook her head. Tears filled her eyes, but didn't fall. She stared up at Gant.

"I give you my word, giant. I will not resist," she quietly promised.

"Magna!" Gabe hissed, struggling to break free.

Gant reached into his pocket and tossed two round, golden collars onto the ground. He pulled a third one out and snapped it around Gabe's throat.

"Place the bands around their necks," Gant instructed. "We will bring them all with us."

"Bands? What bands?" Mike demanded.

"Gant…," Marina protested, a look of horror on her face.

Magna looked at each of them, then at her men. She slowly picked up one of the golden collars with trembling fingers, and locked it around her neck, tears immediately forming in her eyes. She was hiccupping quiet sobs as she put the collar on Kane. Anger began to burn inside Mike at the sight. Whatever these magical collars were, they weren't part of the original plan.

Gant lowered Gabe to the ground. The man immediately went to stand in front of Magna and Kane. Only then did Gant slowly shrink back to his normal size.

"What have you done?" Mike demanded.

Marina marched up to Gant and glared at him with eyes filled with tears. She raised her hand as if to slap him before she turned to Mike and buried her face against him. Mike wrapped his arms around her trembling body.

"He has placed death collars on them," Marina softly explained. "Only he can release them. If they try – if they try to resist him, the collars will tighten until it removes their heads. It is made from the darkest magic known to witches. I – I have never heard of a giant knowing such magic."

Gant returned Mike's glare with cold, hard eyes. Mike had seen this type of look in soldiers who had come back from battles that they never spoke about. "My father was a warlock," Gant replied.

Mike's deep misgivings grew when Gant turned his cold eyes to Marina. "Open the portal," Gant ordered.

"You son-of-a-b—" Gabe started to say when Marina stepped back and whispered the words to open the portal between their worlds.

"We are going to have a talk when we get back," Mike growled.

Gant looked at him and shrugged. "I would do whatever I have to do to save your sister and my future Queen, my King, and my people. Would you have done anything less?" he asked in a solemn voice.

Mike didn't say anything. He watched as Gabe lifted Kane over his shoulder fireman style. Magna walked silently beside her men, her head held high as she stepped through the portal. Gant followed close behind the three. Marina stepped through after Gant, and turned to look at him with a haunted expression. He glanced around the area before shaking his head and stepping through the portal as it began to fade.

On the other side, he wrapped his arm around Marina as they walked. "I won't let anything happen to them," he vowed.

She sniffed. "There may not be anything you can do to save them," she murmured before stepping ahead of him when the path in the garden narrowed.

CHAPTER TWENTY-ONE

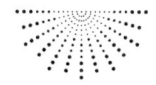

Ruth cursed as she brushed the pollen off of her clothes. A violent sneeze escaped her, causing another shower of pollen to fall from her hair. Whoever thought that pollen was this fine particle that you could barely see had never looked at it up close and personal from the perspective of someone the size of a child's doll.

Bending over at the waist, she ran her hands through her hair trying to shake out all of the pollen that she could. She needed a bath, a shampoo, a drink, and some hot sex – not exactly in that order.

Okay, well, maybe in that order, she grudgingly thought as she saw the thick flakes falling to the ground.

"What I really need is a large dose of magic beans to make me grow," she growled. "Then I would hunt down that miserable piece of shit called LaBluff and show him what happens when he tries to mess with someone his own size!"

Looking around, Ruth realized that if she wanted to get an idea of where she really was, she would need to get higher. She released a soft groan when she saw that the nearest thing to a tree that she could actually climb was a lowly weed. What she needed was a nice, tamed bumblebee or ant like they always seemed to find in the movies.

"This is ridiculous!" she muttered as she walked over to the large weed and began to climb.

Once at the top, she held onto the stem and shaded her eyes with her hand. In the distance, she could see the top of the palace. She moaned in despair – it would take her months to cover that much distance, and that was if she didn't get eaten or trampled along the way.

"Where's the yellow brick road, a flying broomstick, or Santa's sleigh when you need it?" she whispered, staring across the vast terrain.

Releasing a long sigh, she carefully climbed back down. Once she was on the ground, she wiped her palms along the sides of her pants. As much as she might wish it, just standing around wasn't going to get her back to Koorgan. She hunted around for a stick to use as a walking stick or bat to fight off anything that might decide she was breakfast, lunch, or dinner.

"Focus on how many ways you can kill a pirate, Ruth. That will help make the thousands of miles pass more quickly," Ruth grumbled as she struggled up a small mound of dirt.

∼

Koorgan swung off his mount and angrily strode through the palace. He gripped the mirror in his fist. He'd tried to use it a dozen times since Edmond had brought it to him on the docks to no avail.

He took the stairs two at a time until he reached the tower where Ashure was being held. The Pirate King was sitting on the bed with his feet propped up in the chair. The bastard had the nerve to grin at him when he stopped in front of the iron lattice-work door.

Ashure sighed and stood up. He walked over to the door and leaned against it with a slight smirk. Koorgan's fingers curled into a fist. He held out the mirror.

"How does it work?" Koorgan demanded.

Ashure shifted from one foot to the other and grimaced. "Well, you see, that is where there might be a slight problem," he responded with an apologetic grimace.

Koorgan glared at Ashure. "I thought you said it was an enchanted mirror," he snapped.

"Yes, it is. The problem is I'm a pirate. I steal things. Unfortunately, that often leaves me not knowing how some of the items I steal actually work," Ashure explained, glancing down at the mirror before looking back to Koorgan.

"Then how do you know it is enchanted?" Koorgan bit out.

Ashure made an exasperated noise and straightened. "It came from one of the ships belonging to the Isle of Magic. All of their items are enchanted. Unfortunately, they don't come with an instruction manual," he replied with a slight wave of his hand. "You have no idea how dangerous my job can be! Pirates have to be very careful about what we steal – especially from the Isle of Magic. Once, my crew and I were turned into a bunch of Tomcats for a fortnight." Ashure shuddered. "It is not easy sailing a ship with four paws and a tail," he added.

Koorgan pulled his sword from its sheath and held it to Ashure's throat through the bars. Ashure winced and held his hands up in the air. "Of course, I *was* able to get the mirror to work… once."

"Why only once?" Koorgan asked in a deceptively calm voice.

"I unwittingly said the right words, in the right order, it would seem," Ashure muttered.

"And those words are…?" Koorgan asked through clenched teeth as he pressed the sword a little harder.

"Well, I was drunk, so my memory isn't all that clear. We had stolen several very nice cases of brandy destined for the Isle of Monsters. You know that Nali has a love for the stuff. After suffering from the worst hangover in my life – and dealing with the damn sea monkeys Nali sent when she found out that I drank her prized liquor – I've tried to avoid thinking about that particular escapade," Ashure reluctantly confessed.

Koorgan growled. The pirate had to be baiting him. Obviously, he didn't give a damn what condition Ashure had been in, he just wanted to know how to get the mirror to work! Every second he was delayed from finding Ruth was a second that she was in danger. She was probably tired, scared, and wondering if he was ever going to come for her!

"You have until the count of ten to remember. After that, I'll start removing body parts until you do," Koorgan said in a menacing tone.

～

Ashure paled and curled his fingers into his palms when Koorgan moved the blade from his neck to his groin. He was feeling particularly motivated so he fought past the fuzzy filter the wine had imposed on his memories of that night.

It had been a week ago. His ship had raided a small trawler. The merchant had been carrying a wide variety of items from the different kingdoms. The story was embarrassingly boring, in fact, because while Ashure kept up the persona of an indiscriminately dastardly pirate, he was actually very careful about what he stole – and what he bartered for. Yes, he did indeed *barter* – occasionally – with people other than the cantankerous rulers of the Seven Kingdoms.

In this case, the captain of the trawler was a simple merchant trying to support his family, so Ashure had left a small chest of gold and gems in exchange for fresh fruit and vegetables and the mirror. He didn't even know it was enchanted until he inadvertently activated the damn thing. Of course, he would never admit such a thing to Koorgan. Pirates had a very personal and private code of honor, and Ashure made sure that the captains under his command followed that code very carefully – or else they ended up like LaBluff.

But that was neither here nor there. Koorgan was waiting for an answer about the mirror, and he wasn't looking particularly patient. "I was sitting at the table. I'd only had the mirror for a few days. As I mentioned before, such items seldom came with instructions," Ashure murmured, looking at the lone, small table in the room, his eyes narrowed as he remembered that night. He had not started drinking until after he'd held the mirror and it had shown him the thing he treasured the most. He sighed and shook his head.

"What is it?" Koorgan demanded.

"May I sit down? It may trigger my memories," he said, looking at Koorgan.

Koorgan stared at him for a moment before he gave a brief nod and pulled his sword back. Ashure bowed his head in acknowledgement of the reprieve. Walking over to the table, he sat down in one of the chairs, trying to remember the details of the night – or at least the ones he was willing to share.

"The men were celebrating. The ship was filled with barrels of fine wine, fresh fruits and vegetables. It had been a while since they'd had such a feast. The cooks out-did themselves," he shared. "There was very little treasure to be had, but the merchant was also returning with a finely crafted mirror for his lady. He said that it was for his wife. I don't think he realized it was a magical mirror."

"That is all well and good, but it does not tell me how to work the mirror," Koorgan retorted.

Ashure's eyes widened as he started to remember some of the silly rhymes he had been playing with, rhymes that had turned maudlin as he stared into the mirror. "The life of a pirate is good for the sea, but the life of a pirate can make a man bleed," Ashure said, trying to remember the end as he stared into the mirror Koorgan was holding now. "For all the treasure in the world cannot give him the one priceless gem that will warm him within. Oh, magical mirror, grant my wish. Show me the woman that I truly do miss."

Ashure jerked up out of his chair and crossed to the bars. He reached through, grabbing Koorgan's wrist as the mirrored surface began to swirl with color. The colors slowly faded away to show a young woman riding through the woods. Her long hair was unbound and flowing behind her as she gazed back at him in terror. She was holding something in her hand.

When the mirror was suddenly ripped from his hand, Ashure blinked several times to clear his vision. He started to protest before he realized he wasn't back on board his ship; he was in a cell in the palace of the King of the Giants. He watched as Koorgan stepped away from him and over to the window.

"Oh, magical mirror, grant my wish. Show me Ruth who I truly do miss," Koorgan murmured.

A moment later, a look of triumph showed on Koorgan's face. Koorgan reached for the bag the mirror had been in, carefully wrapping the mirror back in it.

"Ready my mount," he ordered Edmond who was standing in the shadows to the right of him.

"What about me?" Ashure demanded when Koorgan started to turn away.

Koorgan paused and stared back at him. "Once she is safe in my arms, then I will have you deposited back on your ship," he informed him.

"Your Majesty, Lord Gant has returned, and he brings the Sea Witch," a guard breathlessly told him.

Ashure watched Koorgan turn and quickly descend the stairs. His attention was not so much focused on the giant as it was on the mirror – the mirror that held the closest thing to hope that he was ever likely to have. He would leave the Isle of the Giants once Ruth returned, but not without the mirror.

∼

Koorgan strode through the corridors, impatient to leave, but he wanted to see Gant first. One of almost a dozen guards standing outside his office quickly opened his office door for him. Koorgan entered, pausing to scan the room.

Magna sat on the settee next to a blond man who was leaning forward with his elbows on his knees. They both looked up when he entered. Another human male, this one almost a large as he was, stood next to the couple. From the male's fierce scowl, cold eyes, and protective stance, Koorgan knew he could be a problem.

Koorgan frowned when he noticed the enchanted collars on the three. He studied Gant, who was standing next to the window. Mike was standing beside the chair where Marina sat across from the three captives.

"Koorgan," Gant greeted in a terse voice. "Have you found Lady Ruth yet?"

"Yes… thanks to Ashure's magic mirror," Koorgan replied, turning to look at Magna.

"What magic did you use on Ruth?" he harshly demanded.

"Watch your tone," the large man coldly stated, taking a step toward Koorgan. "If you can't speak in a nicer tone, I'll kick your ass."

"Gabe…," Magna quietly called, standing and placing a hand on the man's arm before turning to look at him. "I gave her a simple wish spell. All she had to do was make a wish, repeat the words, and it would take her to her brother." She glanced at Mike, and her confusion seemed to be genuine.

The blond man slowly rose to his feet and wrapped his arm around Magna. Koorgan didn't miss the way Magna leaned into the man, her arm secure around his waist to support him as he comforted her. Nor did he miss the fact that her largest protector held her hand. This was not the evil Sea Witch that he remembered. She even looked different. Her frame held a healthy weight and her color was warm, not the sickly sallowness of before. Most different of all, though, was the love shining from her eyes when she looked at her two men.

"Your spell did not take her to Mike, but to the Isle of the Giants. It also shrunk her. You will remain here until I return with her. I want you to analyze the magic and undo it. She later heard a word in the shell that you gave her and returned to normal size for a few hours, but shrank again," Koorgan explained.

"What happens if she can't undo the magic?" the blond man asked.

The muscle in Koorgan's jaw ticked. "Let us hope that I will not have to answer that question," he said before he turned to Gant.

"Stay with them. If they try to escape, use the collars," Koorgan ordered.

"Yes, your Majesty," Gant formally replied with a bow of his head.

Marina took in a deep breath in distress, her eyes wide with horror. He knew that such magic was frowned upon on the Isle of Magic. Even in the darkest of days, the use of such magic had been avoided, and he knew using this type of magic was costing Gant. Unfortunately, he could not risk Magna being able to use her magic – or give her a chance to escape, not until he knew Ruth was normal again.

"Koorgan," Mike called from behind him as he exited the room.

Koorgan turned and patiently waited for Mike. "What is it?" he demanded.

Mike returned his hard gaze. "Ruth would not want you to harm someone else because of her," he said.

Koorgan's eyes darkened with anger. "It may not come to that. I hope it doesn't. Now, I have to go find Ruth," he replied.

"I'm coming with you," Mike said.

Koorgan nodded. "As long as you can keep up," he said, turning and striding down the corridor.

CHAPTER TWENTY-TWO

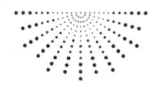

Ruth groaned as she sat down on the rock. Okay, it was really a pebble, but it sure seemed like a huge rock to her at the moment. Her feet hurt, she was thirsty, and somehow she had ended up back at the stupid well where this huge misadventure had started. She reached down, removed her boots, and wiggled her toes.

"Well, not a *huge* misadventure," Ruth murmured, so exhausted that she could barely manage a saucy tone, but the corner of her lips quirked as she amused herself with the irony. She sighed tiredly.

The sound of a soft chuckle caused Ruth to release a startled squeak and she fell off the pebble into the grass. She grunted when she hit the ground. Scrambling to her feet, she picked up her twig and held it out in front of her as she stared up into the face of an old woman.

The woman peered down at her with an amused grin. Ruth narrowed her eyes, thinking about the Wicked Witch who had transformed into the old hag and tantalized Snow White into eating the poisoned apple... though there was also an old hag in another story, one who was actually a beautiful witch – a witch who could have been helpful instead of spiteful if only she'd been offered some kindness. Which story was that again?

Ruth grimaced. She might not be really up to date with her fairy tales, but she knew that things weren't always what they seemed when it came to sweet looking little old ladies.

"Unless you have some magic in that twig, I don't think it will do you much good, my Lady Ruth," the old woman said with a smile.

"Who... Who are you and how do you know who I am?" Ruth demanded, staring up at the woman's wrinkled face and twinkling blue eyes.

The woman sighed and sat down on a rock – a real rock, unlike the pebble Ruth had been sitting on. She stared down at Ruth with a perplexed expression for several minutes before she shook her head again. Bending forward, the woman opened her hand for Ruth to climb onto it.

Ruth lowered the twig, stared at the woman with a raised eyebrow, and firmly shook her head. The story of Hansel and Gretel suddenly popped into her head.

"The kids were never the size of an ant, but there was an old witch in that story as well." Ruth absently muttered to herself.

"I am half Witch, half Giant," the woman replied with another chuckle. Ruth grimaced when she realized that she had spoken aloud. The woman released another sigh and straightened. "My husband, Hermon, is a Giant."

"That still doesn't tell me who you are," Ruth pointed out, waving her twig at the woman.

"No, it doesn't, does it? I am Madura, the Spellbinder – and you are a long, long way from home, my lady," Madura replied with a chuckle.

"Yeah, well, some pirate decided he wanted to make some money by kidnapping me. I happened to have different plans," Ruth replied with a puff of her breath. "Listen, can you help me get back to the palace?"

"There is no need for that, Lady Ruth. Here now, climb into my basket. King Koorgan is on his way, even as we speak. We can have a nice cup of tea while we wait for his Majesty to arrive," Madura assured her.

Ruth stared at the basket Madura held at an angle for her to climb into with an expression of uncertainty. There were several small blue mushrooms nestled in the woven interior. They reminded her of the one that she had spent the night under the first night she was here.

Ruth studied Madura's features. *The woman doesn't look evil. She didn't sound evil, either, but, then, neither did the witch who caught Hansel and Gretel when they were eating her house at first,* Ruth silently reminded herself.

"I am in the King's service, my Lady," Madura said with another sigh. "I cast the spells that protect the history of the kingdom – and a few other things. It is the only magic that I know. Hermon is exceptionally good at growing mushrooms."

"…Okay. I just want you to know that if you try to eat me, I'll give you the nastiest heartburn you'll ever have," Ruth half-teasingly promised.

"I'm sure you would, my Lady," Madura laughed. "Come, King Koorgan shouldn't be much longer."

Ruth bent and picked up her discarded boots. She slipped them on before she awkwardly climbed into the basket and held onto the side as Madura stood up with the help of her cane. As the woman stepped around the deep well where Koorgan had been trapped, Ruth peered down into it, surprised to see that it was now filled with water.

"Where are we going?" Ruth asked.

"To the Spellbinder's cottage. It is just up the path," Madura replied with a smile.

"What… path?" Ruth asked before her mouth dropped open when Madura stepped between two massive trees not ten feet from where they had been sitting. "You've got to be kidding me! I swear that was not here a month ago."

"Of course it was," Madura replied, stepping along the cobblestone path and slowly walking toward the cottage in the middle of the clearing.

"Why didn't you help Koorgan when he fell in the well?" Ruth asked in exasperation, staring at the beautiful, two story cottage that looked more like an old English Inn.

"Because you were the one who was meant to save him, Lady Ruth, not us," Madura replied just before the door to the cottage opened and almost a dozen excited children poured out, running toward them.

~

Koorgan pushed his mount hard. Dirt, gravel, and grass flew behind Genisus's hooves as the battle steed tore down the road. Behind him, a half dozen massive beasts shook the ground with pounding hooves as they raced down the leaf-strewn road. The birds who had gathered to feed on the lush berry-covered bushes flew up into the tall trees, startled.

Two hours later, Koorgan reined in his mount as he neared the old well. Sliding off before the beast stopped completely, he held onto the reins as he desperately scanned the area. Then, wrapping the reins around the horn of his saddle, he reached into the leather bag he had hooked onto it.

The last image from the mirror had shown Ruth being carried in a woven basket. He hadn't been able to see who was carrying her. The mirror had only shown him Ruth.

"Ruth! Ruth!" he called. "Be careful," he ordered his guards. "She is very small. Watch where you step."

"Yes, your Majesty. Spread out. Search everywhere," Edmond ordered.

"Ruth!" Mike called, sliding off his steed.

Koorgan felt around for the cloth bag with the mirror inside it. Pulling it out, he untied the top and he pulled the mirror out. His heart pounded as he held it up.

"Oh, magical mirror grant my wish. Show me the love of my life, show me Ruth," Koorgan murmured.

The silver of the mirror swirled and an image of Ruth, sitting on a thimble and laughing, appeared before him. He couldn't tell exactly where she was, but she looked happy and safe. Relief washed through him.

"Do you see her?" Mike asked.

"Yes, but I don't know where she is yet," Koorgan replied.

Out of his peripheral vision, Koorgan saw his guards spread out. They all took a section and began calling for Ruth with gentle voices, pausing in between to listen. Fear welled up inside Koorgan as several large birds flew overhead. What if one of them, or a different animal, attacked Ruth before he found her? It had happened before with him standing right there.

"Koorgan," Mike called out in a low voice.

Koorgan turned in the direction that Mike was nodding to. His eyes widened when two small children suddenly appeared from between a pair of thick trees. He watched as the little girls hurried over to him and curtsied.

"My King," they both said in unison. Then the slightly taller one looked up at him with glowing hero-worship in her eyes and smiled. "Grandmother asked us to bring you to the cottage."

"Yes, Lady Ruth is there." The other girl giggled. "She is smaller than my dolls."

"Gestelle," the older girl admonished. "Please follow us."

Koorgan's throat tightened as a wave of relief swept through him. He glanced over at Mike and the other guards. Drawing in a deep breath, he nodded to the guards.

"Return to the palace," Koorgan ordered. "Make sure all the pirate ships except for Ashure Wave's are ready to sail the moment I return. Keep him confined to the tower."

"Yes, my King," Edmond said. "I'll personally ensure the rest of the pirates are ready to set sail upon your return."

Koorgan nodded and turned back to follow the two little girls who were whispering and giggling as they gazed in wide-eyed wonder at Mike. An amused smile curved his lips when the youngest girl's eyes widened, and she blushed and giggled again. He had a feeling Mike had given her a wink.

"This way, my King," the oldest girl said, waving to him and Mike.

Koorgan wasn't sure what to expect, but it wasn't the path that suddenly appeared between the two huge trees. Mike released a low whistle of appreciation. They followed the girls a short distance until they reached a sunny meadow with a large cottage nestled in the center.

Outside, a dozen children raced after dogs, chickens, and each other. Several men paused to watch as he walked toward the cottage. One of the men, slightly older than the others, stepped closer to him and bowed.

"King Koorgan, welcome to our home," the man said with a warm smile. "My name is Hermon. I am the protector of these woods and all that grows here. My wife is Madura, the Spellbinder. These are our children and grandchildren."

"Hermon," Koorgan greeted, glancing toward the open door of the cottage. "My Lady Ruth…"

"Of course, my King. Please, follow me," Hermon hastily said with a wave of his hand.

As if by magic, the children stepped to the side, clearing the path leading into the cottage. Mike chuckled softly when the boys gave a stiff bow and the girls did a deep curtsy as they passed. Koorgan briefly paused when a little girl of about three stepped up and handed him a wilted bouquet of wildflowers before she curtsied, giggled, and ran to hide behind an older sibling.

"I think Ruth might have a little competition," Mike teased.

"I won't tell if you don't," Koorgan murmured, feeling more lighthearted now that he knew Ruth was safe.

He nodded to Hermon when the older man bowed and waited for him to precede him. Striding forward, Koorgan stepped into the brightly lit home of Hermon and Madura. His gaze swept the neat, clean area before focusing on the long, polished, wooden dining table.

"Koorgan," Ruth cried out with joy, rising from where she had been sitting on a thimble. "You found me."

Relief flooded Koorgan as he stepped forward and gently scooped up Ruth in his hand. Lifting his hand, he heard her gasp at the sudden change in height and he grimaced. He held his other hand up so that she could step onto it.

"You are unharmed?" Koorgan asked in a low voice.

"Oh, I'm fine. But, once I'm big again, I'm so going to kick me some pirate ass," Ruth said with a relieved laugh.

Koorgan chuckled when Ruth did a one-two punch movement as if she was boxing. He wished with all his heart that he could hold her in his arms. He wanted – needed – to feel for himself that she was alright.

"I don't think that will be necessary. Ashure took care of LaBluff. He will never bother you again." He smiled. "I just wish…." He turned to look at the Spellbinder. "There was a mushroom…." he said.

"Yes, just a moment, please," Madura acknowledged.

Koorgan watched as the old woman waved her hand to one of the young girls standing to the side. The girl nodded and hurried outside. A few minutes later, she returned with a small mushroom lying on a thin piece of cloth. Taking the mushroom from the girl, Madura whispered her thanks before holding out the tiny blue, green, and brown fungus to Koorgan.

"Lady Ruth, please take a bite," Madura encouraged with a gentle smile at Ruth.

Koorgan knelt down on one knee and carefully lowered Ruth to the floor. Once she had stepped off his hand, he held the mushroom out to her. Ruth stepped closer, leaned forward, and took a small bite of the soft, fleshy meat. Koorgan's eyes widened when Ruth began to shimmer.

"Eat more, Ruth," Koorgan encouraged, forcing his hand to remain steady as she took another bite.

By the time she had eaten a dozen bites, her whole body was glowing. Koorgan rose when the swirling golden-white light intensified. Ruth raised her hands in front of her face to watch the light becoming brighter. Excitement and awe at the wondrous magic held Koorgan captive in its beauty. He almost fell backwards when Ruth began to grow.

"Oh!" Ruth exclaimed as she shot upward.

"Oh, dear!" Madura muttered when she realized that she had forgotten something important. "Get my shawl, child."

Ruth blinked several times as Koorgan's arms suddenly wrapped tightly around her. A round of soft snickers drew her attention to the sudden feeling of being very….

"Where are my clothes?" Ruth whispered in horror when she realized that she was standing as naked as the day she was born in front of Madura, Hermon, and almost a dozen of their extended family members.

"Here, Lady Ruth," Madura chuckled, wrapping her long white shawl over Ruth's bare shoulders.

Koorgan ignored everyone. His full attention was focused on Ruth's beautiful face. He cupped her jaw and captured her lips with his, kissing her deeply, passionately, and with a reverence that told her of his love and fear. He slowly pulled away to stare down at her.

"I love you, Ruth Hallbrook," Koorgan whispered. "Now, we can be together forever."

"I love you, too, Koorgan," Ruth replied with a happy smile. "I guess this means no more shrinking?"

Koorgan chuckled. "I certainly hope not," he murmured before kissing her.

"I fear the magic of the mushroom will not last, your Majesty," Madura said with a shake of her head.

"What?" Ruth asked, her eyes filling with tears of frustration, fear, and hopelessness.

Koorgan looked at Madura. "If she continues to eat the mushrooms…," he started to say, stopping when the Spellbinder sadly shook her head.

"The magic affecting Lady Ruth must be removed. The mushrooms will become less and less effective against it. You must find the witch who cast the spell. Only she can remove the spell that continues to affect her Ladyship," Madura said.

"Magna…," Mike said, looking at Koorgan.

"But she is back…," Ruth bit off her protest when she saw the grim determination in Koorgan's eyes.

"She is at the palace. I had Gant retrieve her from your world. She will remove the curse on you or I will remove her head," Koorgan vowed before he turned to look at Madura. "How long does Ruth have before the effects of the mushroom wear off?"

Madura took several of the small mushrooms. "A few hours at most. The magic surrounding Lady Ruth is very strong. Take these," she instructed, wrapping several of the small mushrooms in a white cloth.

"The magic of the forest is fading, your Majesty. If you do not take a bride soon, I fear the few remaining mushrooms will disappear as well," Hermon added.

"That will not happen," Koorgan assured the older man. "We need to return to the palace."

"Dorella, please help Lady Ruth find some clothing," Madura instructed.

The teenage girl smiled and nodded. She motioned for Ruth to follow her. Koorgan tucked the wrap Ruth was wearing more securely around her body and traced his fingers along her cheek.

"I'll be right back," Ruth murmured, pressing a kiss to his lips.

Koorgan nodded. He waited until Ruth had stepped from the room before he looked at Madura. Behind her, he noticed Hermon waving his hand at the children, indicating that everyone should leave the room.

Hermon turned to him with a grave expression and stepped closer to wrap his arm around Madura. Koorgan could see the love between the two and wondered if he and Ruth looked at each other the same way. The thought made him think of his own parents.

"I am doing the best I can to protect the Giants' mushrooms, your Majesty, but even with Madura's magic, they are not growing. To understand the magic behind the giants' ability to grow, you have to understand the mushrooms. The ones that we protect are the original ones planted by the Goddess. They are the source of all the other mushrooms. Within the protection of this forest, under my tender care and Madura's spells, we have been able to protect them from the blight that is slowly taking over the Isle. Even so, the mushrooms are producing fewer and fewer spores to repopulate the supply. The mushrooms she gave you are a fraction of their normal size," Hermon gravely admitted.

"I am aware of the issue. I... am working on rectifying it," Koorgan promised.

"Thank you for your understanding, your Majesty," Hermon replied.

"I know the issue is not with your and Madura's care, Hermon," Koorgan reiterated.

He turned when Ruth reappeared. She was dressed in a pair of dark brown pants, a tan blouse and soft leather shoes. His heart melted when she gave him a smile that wasn't quite steady.

I love you, she mouthed.

He opened his arms and she closed the distance between them. He embraced her tightly and pressed a kiss to the top of her head when she buried her face against him. A shudder ran through his body when she fisted her hands in his shirt along his lower back as if she'd never let him go.

"Let me get you back to the palace and we'll see what the Sea Witch can do about removing the spell," he murmured.

She nodded and took in a shuddering breath before she pulled away. She smiled at Mike, who was silently watching them. Mike opened his arms. Koorgan let her go when she released a sob.

"I'm sorry, sis," Mike said as they embraced.

Ruth shook her head. "I'm giving you a dozen puppies for Christmas," she vowed on a hiccup.

Mike chuckled. "Charlie – and Marina's brother and sisters – will love having the company. Maybe we'll be even again, then," he teased.

She shook her head. "Not by a long shot, baby brother. Wait until your birthday," she threatened.

"Koorgan, I think it's time to go before she can add any more holidays to my punishment," Mike laughed.

"Thank you, Madura – Hermon. Who is Charlie?" Koorgan asked as they turned to exit the house.

"A fluffy, pooping, peeing, floppy-eared piranha that cuts his teeth on your brand new furniture," Mike answered.

"Puppies aren't that bad," Ruth defended.

Mike shook his head. "Don't believe her," he solemnly advised as he mounted his steed.

Koorgan laughed. He'd been unable to keep his hands off of Ruth as they left the cottage, and now he lifted her onto Genisus, handing her the precious handkerchief of mushrooms before he mounted behind her. Wrapping an arm around her waist, he made sure she was comfortable before he tapped Genisus's sides.

"Let's go. We have a spell to break," he said.

CHAPTER TWENTY-THREE

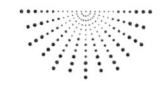

The journey back to the palace was interrupted twice when Ruth began to glow. The magic of the mushrooms was lasting a shorter time than Madura had predicted. Koorgan felt Ruth sag back against him in exhaustion.

"How are you doing?" he asked.

She leaned her head back against his shoulder. "I feel like a convoy of semis – think a hundred Genisuses – have run over me, backed up, and did it again about a hundred times," she admitted.

Koorgan regretted that LaBluff wasn't still alive so he could kill him. Ruth should have been safe in his own bedroom, not lost and fighting for survival somewhere in the countryside. He didn't truly know what had happened to the pirate or what kind of magic the Pirate King had, but after seeing what he'd witnessed, he would never again look at Ashure as the fun-loving pirate that he projected to the world. Ashure was a serious threat.

If Magna was unable to reverse the spell on Ruth, he might barter with Ashure to end the Sea Witch's life in exchange for the pirate's freedom.

Regardless, both would be gone from the Isle of the Giants one way or another before the sun set this evening.

Two hours later, he helped Ruth down from Genisus, sweeping her up into his arms when her legs threatened to collapse under her. She wrapped her arm around his neck, and he carried her up the front steps into the palace. After striding up the second set of steps with Mike by his side, they walked down the long corridor to his office. The guards outside straightened to attention. The guard standing closest to the door hurriedly opened it.

"Koorgan! Lady Ruth…," Gant said, rising from the table where he had been sitting.

"Mike," Marina said, her voice filled with relief.

Koorgan carried Ruth over to the couch. Magna, Gabe, and Kane all rose as he approached. He hadn't missed Magna's murmur of concern when she saw Ruth. He gently laid Ruth down on the sofa.

"Ruth," Magna softly exclaimed, kneeling next to her.

Koorgan wrapped his fingers around Magna's wrist when she started to reach for Ruth. Both Gabe and Kane swore under their breaths. Gant rose when they moved to stop Koorgan, and both men fell to their knees, clawing at the collars around their necks. Magna's anguished cry filled the room.

"Please – I only want to help her. Don't hurt them," Magna begged, turning to look at Gant with an imploring gaze.

Koorgan shot Gant a look and shook his head. Gant slowly lowered his hand. Kane leaned forward, gasping for breath while Gabe muttered a long string of threats. Koorgan admonished the big man.

"You are not helping the situation," he stated.

"You take this fucking magic dog collar off and I'll show you how I can rectify this situation," Gabe retorted.

"Gabe, will you shut up? I don't have the same death wish that you do," Kane groaned.

"Please, your Majesty, don't hurt them. I need a moment with Ruth to find out what happened," Magna said in a low, urgent voice.

"Gant, stand down," Koorgan ordered, releasing Magna's wrist. "Help her, Sea Witch, but know this – if anything happens to her, I will show neither you nor your men any mercy. Do you understand?"

Magna tilted her head and looked at him. "Yes," she replied.

Koorgan stepped back and nodded to her. Kane staggered to his feet and gripped Gabe's forearm, pulling him back. The room grew silent except for Magna's soft voice.

"Ruth, when you used the shell, tell me exactly what happened," Magna requested.

Ruth's eyelashes fluttered and she gave Magna a tired smile. "'All hell broke loose' would be an apt description. Let me tell you something, you do not want to say the damn words wrong. It was hard enough to understand them in the first place, but even harder with Agents Maitland and Tanaka arguing in the background," she said.

Magna frowned. "There were others with you?" she asked.

Ruth nodded and closed her eyes. "Yes. Asahi knew about the Seven Kingdoms from his grandfather. He had information I wanted and I wasn't opposed to having a trained CIA agent watching my back while I was in Fantasyland. He followed me to the beach. What we didn't know was the FBI agent had been following us. I was in the middle of saying the spell when she appeared. I said the last word wrong and then corrected it, but the next thing I knew, I was a Lilliputian stuck on the Isle of the Giants. I stumbled upon Koorgan, and the rest is history. God, but I'm so tired. I need a nap before I declare war on the pirates," she mumbled.

Magna laughed. Koorgan frowned down at the Sea Witch. He didn't find anything about the situation funny. His faint growl of disapproval caught Magna's attention and she looked up at him with a wary expression.

"Can you help her?" he snapped impatiently.

"Yes. The combination of her mispronouncing the final word and the strain on the spell caused by the additional people corrupted it. It would help if I had the shell that I gave her. The spell and the memories of everything that happened will have been captured inside it," Magna replied.

"It's in the dollhouse in the jewelry box on the nightstand," Ruth murmured.

"I will return with it," Koorgan said.

Magna nodded. Koorgan quickly exited the room. It would be faster for him to retrieve the item than to instruct anyone else. He took the stairs leading up to his quarters three at a time. Guards and servants watched him pass with a worried expression.

He entered his quarters and hurried to the master bedroom. Striding across the room to the dollhouse, he carefully opened the side of it and reached for the tiny jewelry box on the vanity. He opened the box with his fingernail. A sigh of relief swept through him when he saw the red shell nestled inside. He closed the box and retraced his steps.

A minute later, he was re-entering his office. Everyone straightened when he entered. He walked toward Magna and held out the jewelry box. She took it from him, opened it, and tilted the box until the shell fell into the palm of her hand.

"I will need to have the collar removed if I am to use my magic to undo the damage," she said, looking from him to Gant.

"Very well," Koorgan agreed.

"Koorgan – if I remove the collar…," Gant started to protest.

Koorgan looked at Gant. "If she tries anything, kill her men," he ordered.

Gant's lip pursed before he gave a nod of understanding. With a wave of his hand, the glow on Magna's golden collar faded and the lock released. She reached up with one hand and removed it, dropping it to the floor with a shudder.

She rose to her feet next to the couch and held the shell over Ruth's limp body. Her soft whispers filled the room. Koorgan watched as she turned her hand over and opened it. The shell within her grasp was no longer tiny, but the size of a large piece of fruit.

"Show me what happened," Magna commanded.

Vivid images with sound played out as if Magna had projected what had happened on the beach. Koorgan saw a tall, slender man standing near Ruth. He heard Marina's soft gasp.

"That is Agent Asahi Tanaka," Mike shared.

Ruth was talking to the man who nodded in understanding. She kept lifting the red shell to her ear as they walked down the beach. Then Ruth suddenly froze as she heard something in the shell.

"That is where I opened the portal," Marina murmured.

Magna nodded. "I told her the shell would lead her to Mike's last location before he left his world," she said.

A moment later, a young woman came running down the beach, her shoulder-length dark hair streaming behind her. Asahi turned and frowned. The woman didn't stop until she was standing in front of him. The sound of her voice was drowned out by the swirl of magic suddenly engulfing Ruth. Both the woman and Asahi turned and reached for Ruth at the same time as she stumbled over the last word of the spell.

Magna's hand began to move through the projected image. Koorgan could suddenly see the actual threads of magic. Magna was untangling them. Her hands wove through the colors as she murmured a series of chants. As each thread was untangled, it disappeared.

"I've only ever seen this type of power in a witch once before – Queen Magika," Marina breathed in awe.

"Gant, what about you?" Koorgan asked.

"This is very powerful magic, Koorgan, but what she is doing is correct," Gant responded.

"You show them how real magic is done, sweetheart," Gabe added.

"It's like watching a surgeon in action," Kane reflected.

"Only a lot cooler and less bloody," Gabe retorted.

Koorgan stepped forward in alarm when Ruth's body suddenly bowed up on the couch and she released a strangled cry. A familiar shimmering glow covered her body, the same glow that he had noticed surrounding her before she shrank. Fear choked him as he watched the light intensify before it swirled like water going down the drain, and it disappeared into the shell. When the last bit of the magic poured into the shell, it exploded in a brilliant fireball of gold, red, and white lights.

Ruth sank back against the couch and relaxed. Magna stepped back from the couch and turned to look at him with a smile. As he looked into her brilliant green eyes, he could see her exhaustion – and her resignation.

"I have done as you asked. I will take whatever punishment you wish to deliver to me without protest. All that I ask is for your man to release Gabe and Kane from the collars and that you ensure they are safely returned to their world," she requested.

The two men loudly expressed their displeasure with that plan, but Magna just lifted her chin. Koorgan's gaze moved to Ruth where she lay peacefully against the cushions.

"Oh, for crying out loud," Ruth said, opening her sparkling eyes and smiling up at Koorgan. "Let them all go back! At least it will eliminate the creative litany of salty sailor's language," Ruth commented with a wink at the swearing sailors in question.

"Gant, release the men," Koorgan ordered, his focus locked on Ruth.

"Are you sure? I swear the big one wants to beat your ass," Gant warned.

Koorgan shot Gabe a quick look. The human was rubbing his fist against his palm. At this point, he would take his chances.

"I'll let you deal with him if he tries," Koorgan replied.

Gant muttered a few salty words of his own before he deactivated the collars and unlocked them. Both men immediately tore the devices off their necks and tossed them to the floor before pulling Magna protectively between them with hostile glares at Gant and Koorgan.

"Can we leave?" Gabe demanded.

"Yes, the agreement has been fulfilled," Koorgan said.

"I'll open a portal for you," Marina volunteered, stepping forward.

"Thank you. I only know one way back, and unfortunately, it would be too dangerous for Gabe and Kane to journey that way," Magna said.

"I can teach you the spell if you like – just in case you ever need it," Marina hesitantly murmured.

Magna lovingly looked at Gabe and Kane, then glanced at Koorgan and regretfully shook her head.

"I'm not sure that would be a good idea," Magna replied.

"You never know," Marina softly responded.

Magna nodded to the young witch. "I… never had a chance to thank you and Mike for what you did," she said.

Mike stepped closer and looked down at Magna. "The Seven Kingdoms owe you the thanks, Magna. Without your sacrifice, things could have been much, much worse," he reminded her.

"Okay, enough with the long goodbyes. How do we get the hell out of here?" Gabe interjected.

Kane shook his head. "Really nice, such finesse, Gabe. Remind me the next time you need sutures to use a bigger needle," he retorted.

"Super glue is better," Ruth and Gabe automatically responded at the same time.

Mike chuckled. Koorgan caught Gant's eye and nodded to the door. He wanted – needed – some quiet time alone with Ruth. Gant rounded them all up and herded them toward the door. Ruth opened her eyes again and smiled up at him when the door closed behind the animated group.

He stepped over to the couch and sank down on the edge of it. They reached for each other at the same time. Warm tears dampened the flesh along his throat and he heard Ruth sniff.

"How do you feel?" he asked, pulling back to look down at her.

She chuckled, sniffed, and wiped her cheek. "Terrified, exhilarated, horny, shaky," she listed in between sniffs.

"Did you say horny?" he murmured, cupping her chin.

She gave him a watery grin. "I was checking to see if you were listening," she joked.

"Oh, I'm listening," he promised, crowding closer to her.

Her hands ran up his arms to his shoulders. "Is there a lock on the door?" she whispered against his lips.

CHAPTER TWENTY-FOUR

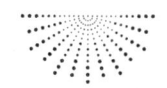

Later that evening, Koorgan watched as Ruth dried her hair with one hand and lovingly touched the dollhouse with her other. She reached in and pulled the covers over the bed. He finished buttoning his shirt and walked over to her, sliding his hands along her hips. Leaning down, he brushed a kiss against her throat.

"Are you sure you want to go downstairs?" he asked.

She chuckled and turned in his arms. "Considering that my brother and Marina came all this way to see me and I've spent like zero time with them, I think it might be nice to at least have dinner with them – especially now that the pirates are gone," she replied, sliding her arms around his neck.

"Pirates…. Ashure!" Koorgan groaned.

"What's wrong?" Ruth asked.

"Ashure is still locked in the tower. I forgot about him," he replied.

"What about the ass that kidnapped me? I hope he spent a little time in the tower," she said with a distasteful wiggle of her nose.

Koorgan grimaced. "He is dead," he said, gripping her hands in his.

She looked at him in shock. "Dead? But... I mean... I just wanted his ass kicked! He didn't deserve to die, Koorgan," she whispered in shock.

"I did not kill him, Ashure did, but not before he forced LaBluff to admit what he'd done. How Ashure killed him is another matter, but the reason for it is because he betrayed Ashure, intending that I would blame the Pirate King for your disappearance, and kill him. A betrayal like that cannot be ignored, Ruth – not with the power that each kingdom holds. Without Ashure's help, it would have taken much longer to find you," he explained.

"Still...." She shook her head.

He cupped her chin. She tilted her head back and he brushed a firm kiss across her lips. He ached to take away the haunted look in her eyes.

"Our worlds aren't that different in some ways," she conceded.

"I look forward to hearing about how they are both the same and different. I guess I should invite the Pirate King to dinner since I kept him locked up all day – unless you'd rather I didn't," Koorgan added.

"He helped you find me?" she asked, biting her lower lip.

"Yes," he grudgingly admitted.

"Well, it wouldn't be a very nice 'thank you' to put him on his ship without dinner – maybe we can send him off without dessert, but that is open for negotiation," she decided.

Koorgan chuckled. "I like the way you think," he said.

"You'd better, because I would love...," her voice faded when she looked down at Koorgan as he got down on one knee, holding both of her hands.

"I planned on waiting until after dinner, but I don't want to wait any longer," he began.

"Koorgan...," Ruth whispered.

"Ruth Hallbrook, I am asking you not only as the King of the Giants, not just for my people or for my kingdom, but for me – from my heart – will you accept me and agree to be my wife first and the Queen of our people for now and forever? I love you, Ruth. I want and need to be with you. You are my heart – my—"

Ruth cut his words off before he could finish. Her lips captured his as she threw herself into his arms, wrapping her arms around his neck. He lowered her to the rug next to their bed and deepened their kiss. Her lips eagerly parted.

He finally pulled back, brushing a series of kisses along her lips and jaw. Her hands threaded through his hair and she gazed up at him. A soft groan rumbled in his throat when he saw her desire laden eyes.

"Yes," she murmured. "Yes, I'll marry you. Yes, I'll be there for you. Yes, I'll love you forever and ever, and save you from contracts and accounting, and be your... Queen."

He pressed a kiss to the corner of her eye, catching the tear that escaped, nuzzled his head against her neck, and closed his eyes. A powerful emotion swept through him and he knew it was the balance the Goddess had said was needed to rule his kingdom. This is what she meant – love. With love came hope and promise.

"I love you, Ruth," he said in a hoarse voice filled with emotion.

"I know, Koorgan. I can feel it," she whispered, turning her head and looking at him with a mischievous grin as she slid her hand down between them to his engorged cock.

He chuckled and lifted his head. "Not as much as you will later," he said, suddenly rolling so that she was lying on top of him.

"We're procrastinating , aren't we?" she reflected with a sigh.

"Maybe... a little," he agreed, working on the buttons on her blouse.

"Well, they say it is always good to be fashionably late if you want to make a grand entrance," she muttered, sitting up, pulling her blouse off, and tossing it to the side before reaching for her bra.

"I like the late part," Koorgan murmured.

He cupped her breasts and sat up enough to capture one taut nipple between his lips. She leaned forward, pressing him back against the floor. They might make it to the bed – or they might not, he thought.

∽

Ruth ignored Mike's amused look when they finally made it down to the sitting room almost an hour late. Ashure turned and gave her a wry smile. Koorgan had directed Gant to release Ashure from the tower while she was getting dressed for the second time that evening.

"Lady Ruth, it is a pleasure to see that you are once again yourself, though I'm sure you would have been a delightful sight in your other form as well," Ashure commented.

"Brandy, Ashure?" Koorgan inquired.

"That would be nice," Ashure replied.

"It should be – it came from your ship," Gant informed him.

A pained expression crossed Ashure's face. "You do know that stash was for the Empress, don't you? Nali is not going to be happy if I don't have a goodwill gesture for her," he complained aloud, but still took the glass of fine brandy.

"Nali will forgive you. For some reason, she seems to have a soft spot for you," Koorgan said.

"Most women do," Ashure quipped with a smile at Ruth.

She looked at him with a raised eyebrow. Ashure grimaced and turned his smile on Marina who smiled back at him. Ruth rolled her eyes when he beamed, and crossed over to chat with Mike and Marina.

"I like the way you do that little expression of scorn touched with a 'drop dead' look," Gant chuckled.

Ruth grinned. "There have been a lot of men for me to practice it on," she said.

"May I escort you into the dining room, my Lady?" Koorgan asked.

Koorgan could melt her heart so easily, the way he stepped in front of her, looking so handsome, held out his hand, and bowed. It was enough to make her go weak in her already wobbly knees. The man was potent when he was on a roll.

"Yes," she murmured, placing her hand in his.

Gant looked back and forth between them, and Ruth felt his gaze move to her left hand and the glittering ring on her finger. A slow grin grew on his face.

"You asked her," he exclaimed.

Koorgan returned his grin. "I asked her. The ceremony will be tomorrow morning. We both agreed that we wanted a simple union first and will hold a larger one in a month's time," he said.

"Congratulations, my Queen," Gant said with a formal bow.

Ruth leaned over and brushed a kiss against Gant's cheek. "Thank you, Gant, for everything," she said.

Gant bowed his head again. "Any time, my Queen," he murmured.

Ruth turned and walked beside Koorgan. They were eating in the informal dining room which had a smaller, round table. She looked up and smiled at Mike. He returned her smile with one of his own.

Congratulations, sis, he mouthed.

All she could do was beam. She was surprised that no one complained about the bright glow because she was pretty sure that she was currently competing with all the stars in the universe. She looked around the table. Ashure was entertaining Marina and Mike with wild tales of his exploits while Gant was adding a running commentary of said exploits while their audience dissolved into fits of laughter.

This is what real magic is, Ruth thought. *Friends, families – and the occasional irritating pirate.*

"I'd like to make a toast to Koorgan and Ruth," Gant suddenly announced, standing up and holding up his glass of brandy. "To the future Queen of the Giants and our beloved King."

"To the future Queen and King of the Giants," Mike, Marina, and Ashure toasted.

"And to wishes, dreams, and future prosperous trade agreements," Ashure slipped in as everyone sipped their drinks, leading to more laughter.

~

Two hours later, the group had adjourned to the sitting room. Mike and Marina were curled up on one couch while Ruth and Koorgan sat on the other. Gant and Ashure sat in the chairs across from them. Koorgan listened as Ashure and Gant talked quietly about the different kingdoms.

"The only one I have yet to visit more than once is the Isle of the Elementals. They are a strange species," Ashure was saying.

"My parents disappeared on a visit there," Koorgan said without thinking.

Ashure turned and looked at him with a frown. "I assumed they had given over the kingdom to you so they could travel. When did this happen?" he inquired.

Koorgan shrugged. "Shortly after the Great War ended – after the dragons were turned to stone," he replied.

"The Isle of the Elementals rose above the seas during that time. Is it possible they were trapped on it?" Ashure asked.

"I don't know. I sent investigators throughout the kingdoms right after their disappearance. Nothing was ever found. I suspected that the Sea Witch attacked and killed them, but there was never any proof. Knowing what I know now about what happened to her, I should have asked Magna whether the alien creature had anything to do with their disappearance. Perhaps I can pay her a visit soon," he said.

"What about the mirror?" Mike asked.

Koorgan looked at Mike. "The mirror?" he repeated.

Mike nodded. "It showed you where Ruth was. Is it possible it could help you locate your parents?" he asked.

Koorgan turned his gaze back to Ashure. "Is it possible?" he questioned.

Ashure shrugged. "If it is your heart's desire to learn their fate, I suspect the mirror could show you where they are – if they are still alive," he said.

Koorgan stood up. "I'll return in a moment," he murmured.

Koorgan quickly exited the sitting room and returned to his living quarters. He retrieved the magic mirror, pulled it out of the bag, and held it in front of him.

"Mirror, show me where my parents are," he ordered.

Nothing happened. Then he remembered the correct phrase for this mirror.

"Oh magical mirror, grant my wish, show me my parents," Koorgan said impatiently.

The image on the mirror swirled. Vivid colors of pearlescent pinks, whites, and blues created a mist. Koorgan frowned as he tried to understand what the mirror was showing him. A second later, the mist thinned and he saw his parents embracing as if they feared for their lives. They seemed to have been frozen as they turned, braced for an attack. It took a moment for Koorgan to realize that the figures were formed from two trees, their features immobile in the bark.

Frustrated, he placed the mirror back in the bag and exited his rooms.

He returned to the sitting area. Everyone stopped chatting and looked at him.

"What do you make of this?" he asked without preamble, holding up the mirror and repeating the correct phrase. The mirror again reached through multicolored mists to show the trees with his parents' features.

Mike, Marina, Ruth, Gant, and Ashure all rose to gather around him as the mirror revealed the image of his parents. Marina's eyes widened and she gasped. Koorgan's gaze pierced her, but Marina's attention remained locked on the image.

"It *is* the Isle of the Elementals. I… There are tales – myths really, that the King and Queen can turn creatures into different elements. No one ever really believed it. We always thought that such tales were spread to cause fear. I mean, who wants to be turned to stone or water… or plants?" she said, her voice dropping to a whisper on the last two words.

"Plants? Are you saying these trees are – they are actually my parents?" Koorgan asked in an incredulous tone.

Marina nodded. "Yes. No one knows for sure where the Isle of the Elementals is located," she said.

Ashure nodded. "I have sailed the oceans and have only visited the Isle once – long, long ago before it floated out of the ocean. I have never seen it again," he agreed.

Koorgan looked down at the mirror. "Oh magical mirror, grant my wish. Show me where the Isle of the Elementals is located," he ordered.

The image on the mirror swirled, but the only thing that appeared was a heavy mist. No matter how hard he tried, the Isle's location was concealed from view – even from the powerful magic of the mirror. He finally lowered the mirror, his mind deep in thought.

Koorgan looked up when Ruth slid her arm around him, and he sighed, carefully placing the mirror back into the bag. He placed it on the small table near the couch. The others returned to their seats.

"We know they are alive," Gant reassured. "I can form a team and lead it myself to find them, Koorgan," he offered.

Koorgan frowned. "What are you going to look for – mist?" he asked.

Gant shrugged. "It is a start," he said.

"The question is how do you break the magic once they are found? It would take the King and Queen of the Elementals to reverse such a spell, much like it took Magna to reverse the spell on Ruth," Marina added.

"Could Queen Magika or King Oray reverse the spell?" Koorgan asked.

Marina shook her head. "No, the magic of the Isle of Magic is not tied to the elements, it is tied to the energy inside and surrounding us," Marina explained.

"Good luck finding it," Ashure said. "As I said, I've sailed all the oceans and what you seek is never in the same place twice." He yawned. "It would appear that captivity is exhausting. I think it is time for me to retire to my empty ship, hope no more of my crew attempts to mutiny since they no longer have any cargo to sell, and search for more lucrative deals."

"You can stay the night. I'll have Edmond arrange to return your cargo tomorrow – minus a case of the brandy," Koorgan said.

Ashure grinned. "Well, in that case, perhaps another glass wouldn't hurt before I call it a night," he replied, rubbing his hands.

EPILOGUE

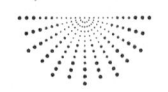

"According to the inventory list, that is everything," Ruth called out to Dapier, Ashure's acquisitions agent aboard his ship.

"Except for three cases of the finest, most magical brandy ever produced by the best craftsmen in the Seven Kingdoms," Ashure added under his breath.

"Consider it a restocking fee," Ruth lightly quipped.

"Restocking! Koorgan was the one who had everything taken off in the first place," Ashure argued.

"And he can do it again," Koorgan threatened as he walked along the dock. "Or better yet, he can take the whole damn ship, give you the rowboat, and send you and your men on their merry way."

Ruth's lips twitched with amusement when she saw a muscle jump in Ashure's jaw as he tried to keep from making the situation worse. The pirate's gaze moved from Koorgan to his ship and he loudly sighed. She had a feeling that Ashure was going to be glad to leave the Isle of the Giants.

"Can I at least have my mirror back?" Ashure requested.

"Consider it a thank-you-for-not-killing-me fee," Koorgan replied.

Ashure shot Koorgan a heated glare. "You are absolutely no fun to negotiate with anymore! Fees, ridiculous charges – I hope you know that I'm going to have to increase my own prices because of you," he sniffed in indignation.

"I'm still deciding whether to allow you to return to my Isle. I think this mirror is a miniscule price to pay for keeping your neck from hanging along the north cliffs," Koorgan replied.

Ashure's eyes swept over the bag that Koorgan held up, and he suddenly smiled. Ruth frowned when Ashure good-naturedly slapped Koorgan on the shoulder. The sudden mood change almost gave her whiplash.

"Yes, yes, you are a fearsome giant I could hardly hope to best, lowly pirate that I am. I am grateful for my life. Perhaps if I'm in the area, I can stop by for your wedding in a month's time. If not, I wish you all the best. Consider the brandy and the mirror a wedding present from the Pirates of the Seven Kingdoms, a goodwill gesture for future trade deals. Now, I believe my men are ready. Lady Ruth, if you ever decide to leave this arrogant giant, I will be but a change in the wind away," Ashure declared with an elegant deep bow and a kiss to the back of her hand.

"Thank you. I'll keep that in mind," she dryly replied.

"I hope you do. Koorgan, an unpleasant experience as usual. I suggest you redecorate your tower. It is very dull and boring," Ashure commented before he stepped back and gave them both another elegant bow.

Ruth watched in amusement as Ashure called out to Dapier to prepare to cast the lines. She wrapped her arm around Koorgan when he slid his arm around her waist. They stood on the docks for a while, watching as the Pirate King's ship sailed out of the harbor.

"Koorgan," Gant called out behind them.

They turned and watched as Gant dismounted from his steed and handed the reins to a dockhand. His furious glare was on the departing ship as he shook his head with resignation and amusement.

"What has he done now?" Koorgan asked.

"Well, you can forget about the brandy. He only left three bottles. The rest of the cases were filled with sea monkeys! The damn things are running amok in the castle. I have the guards catching them to release back into the ocean. The mischievous creatures are going to be hell on the shipping and fishing boats until I can send word to Nali to control them," he replied.

"Sea monkeys? We have those back home. I had some for a while after my disaster with the mice – another gift from Mike. Our sea monkeys are a hybrid breed of brine shrimp. They are actually pretty cool," she remarked.

"These are anything but cool. They love to create chaos. They climb everywhere, and if you aren't careful, they bite," Gant explained.

Just then, Ruth heard a scream. They all turned to see dozens of eight-legged creatures running down the dock chased by a half dozen guards wielding brooms. One sea monkey had stopped to toss a crate while another had lifted up the skirt of a woman, but the stragglers didn't pause for long. They ran, they swung, and they chattered with an almost insane lilt to their voices.

Koorgan grabbed Ruth and pulled her up in his arms as a sea monkey jumped up on Gant's steed while another pushed the poor dock hand, who'd been holding the reins, off the dock into the water.

Gant loudly swore when his horse swept by them, heading for the end of the dock. He lifted his fingers to his mouth and released a loud whistle. The horse slid to a stop, bowing its head, and bucked. The two sea monkeys on its back flew through the air, landing with a great splash in the water.

"Our sea monkeys don't look anything like that," Ruth agreed.

Koorgan turned when several more of the strange creatures, hurried along by guards and merchants, swept by them. She couldn't help but giggle at the comical scene. People were swinging brooms and mops at the riotous sea monkeys. More than one person ended up in the water with the creatures. Ruth gasped when she saw three of the creatures heading for Gant, who had gone to retrieve his horse.

"Gant, look out!" Koorgan yelled.

The warning came a split second too late. Two of the creatures spun Gant around, knocking him off balance while the third one miscalculated his escape. The sea monkey jumped just as Gant threw open his arms in an effort to keep from falling off the end of the dock. The creature landed squarely in the center of Gant's chest. They watched as Gant and the sea monkey disappeared over the edge of the dock into the water.

"Oh my. I hope Gant can swim," she giggled.

Koorgan chuckled. "He can," he said.

"Why are they using brooms and mops?" she asked, watching a woman shoo two more sea monkeys into the water with a mop.

"Nali, the Empress of the Monsters, has an affection for the damn creatures. Since no one wants to upset the Empress of Monsters, it is just easier to chase the creatures back into the water and clean up the mess," Koorgan explained.

Ruth leaned her head against his shoulder. "There is so much that I still have to learn about your world," she reflected.

"Our world, Ruth. This is *our* world," Koorgan gently corrected her.

"Our world – it sure is better not being the size of a doll. I have to say that was an interesting experience I'd rather never have to deal with again," she murmured with a sigh.

"You are not the only one. I think that is the last of them," Koorgan replied, looking around before he gently set her back on her feet.

They both turned and watched as Gant climbed the ladder attached to the dock. Ruth covered her mouth to hide her smile when he shook like a dog, sending water everywhere. He grabbed the reins of his mount when his horse walked over to him. It was impossible not to laugh, especially when he got close enough to them that she could hear the squish of water in his boots and see it seeping out of the leather. He scowled at both of them.

"There is only one thing I hate more than sea monkeys," he growled.

"What is that?" Ruth couldn't resist asking.

"Ashure Waves," Gant grunted, wiggling and reaching into his shirt.

Laughter burst from her and Koorgan when Gant pulled a small fish out of his shirt with a grimace. He threw the fish back into the water, shuddering in disgust, before he turned a heated glare on Koorgan.

"I'm taking the rest of the afternoon off. I'll see you this evening at your ceremony," he muttered.

"See you later, Gant," Ruth snickered.

Koorgan's laugh resonated across the docks, causing some of the crowd to pause and smile. Gant paused midway through mounting his horse, reached into his trousers, and pulled out another small, slender fish. Ruth giggled when Gant muttered a long string of dire threats aimed at Ashure. With a toss of his hand, the wiggling fish landed with a plop on the dock before a child ran over and tossed it back into the water. She released a contented sigh and leaned back against Koorgan when he wrapped his arms around her.

"This is so much more fun than dealing with white-collar knuckle-heads," she murmured.

"How would you like to go back to the palace and deal with a very sexy giant?" Koorgan suggested, pressing a kiss to her neck.

"That sounds like the perfect job for me," she said, turning in his arms and capturing his lips.

∽

"I'm going to kill that damn pirate!" Koorgan snarled as he came into their living quarters later that evening.

"What did Ashure do now?" she laughed as she adjusted the earring she had just stuck through her ear.

"He is a conniving, thieving…," Koorgan growled, shaking the bag with the mirror in it.

Ruth fought back her chuckle at the sound of exasperation in Koorgan's voice. She raised an eyebrow and wondered what could possibly have happened this time. It had already taken all day to restore order to the palace.

"That *is* what pirates are, love," she dryly reminded him as she walked over and wrapped her arms around his neck.

"He took the mirror. I've been carrying around a damn snack tray all day," he grudgingly admitted.

Ruth twisted and watched Koorgan tip the bag. A small silver snack tray fell out of the bag into his hand. She covered her mouth with her hand to keep from laughing.

"Well, that explains why he was in such a hurry to leave when he saw you carrying the bag and you refused to give it back to him," she said.

"Yes. In all the confusion with the sea monkeys, I didn't bother checking the bag. I should have known he would never leave without it," he confessed.

Ruth tenderly caressed his cheek. "How badly will this affect Gant's search for your parents?" she asked with concern.

"Very little. The mirror cannot show us the Isle's location. The only way to find the Isle of the Elementals is to search for it. Gant is going to approach Nali, Drago, and Orion to see if they would be willing to assign some members from their Isles to help," he said.

"I remember who Nali is. She's the Empress of the Monsters, isn't she? Who are Drago and Orion again?" she asked.

"Yes, Nali is the Empress of the Monsters. Drago is the King of the Dragons and Orion is the King of the Sea People. With their help, Gant can expand the search. I have no doubt that Ashure will also help – in his own way. If for nothing else, to get back into my good graces," he said.

Ruth nodded. "I hope they find them. It seems with so many searching, it is only a matter of time before the Isle of the Elementals is found," she observed.

Koorgan caressed her cheek. "Have I mentioned how beautiful you are?" he murmured.

Ruth brushed a kiss across his lips. "Not in the last five minutes. You are very good for my ego in case you didn't realize it," she teased.

"I love you, Ruth. Tonight, I make you my Queen, but in my heart, you will always be my little rescuer. The woman who never gave up, who captured my imagination the moment I saw you standing on the edge of the well with your hands on your hips," he said in a tender voice.

"Let's go get married," she said, gripping his hand tightly in hers.

"As you wish, my Lady," he replied.

Ruth's heart fluttered at his words. Together they paused at the top of the stairs. Mike, Marina, and Gant all stood at the bottom of the staircase with large smiles on their faces. Servants and guards lined the corridors. Ruth smiled when she saw Hermon, Madura, and their dozens of children and grandchildren in attendance.

Ruth looked at her brother. Mike's eyes glittered with pride and love. Tears of emotion filled her eyes when she saw him mouth '*I love you, sis*'. She smiled and mouthed '*I love you more*'.

Her hand tightened on Koorgan's as they slowly descended the staircase to where the Director of Archives stood waiting to join them together in matrimony. There would be another formal ceremony for the entire Kingdom later, but this one meant more to her. A giggle escaped Ruth when a small, mischievous Sea Monkey suddenly peeked out from behind the Director of Archives.

This is my kind of adventure: love, happiness… and the occasional sea monkey, she thought with a glow of contentment.

To be continued…The Magic Shell

Ross stared out at the sea. He needed time to think. He hated to admit it, but at the moment he felt lost. Carefully making his way to the back of his fishing trawler, he checked the nets to make sure they weren't tangled, then he climbed up to check the top lines as well. One of the lines looked like it was twisted and might get caught when he hauled the nets back in.

Holding onto the rope, he stared out at the shimmering water. It wouldn't stay like this for long, clear and sunny. By mid-afternoon, the cold, moist air coming in off the water would hit the warmer surface of the land and a fog would roll across in a thick blanket that was almost impossible to see through.

He drew in a deep breath, held it for several long seconds, then released it. He knew that most of his restlessness came from recent events. There had been a rash of disappearances over the last couple of years. He had known Mike Hallbrook, a detective for the Yachats Police Department, who had disappeared a few months back. They had played pool and enjoyed some beers down at the local pub on rare occasions. There wasn't a hell of a lot else to do in the area except fishing and hiking.

Hell, he had even known Carly Tate and Jenny Ackerly. It was kind-of hard not to know everyone when you lived in a town the size of Yachats, Oregon. His restlessness had come to a head when his mother had died a week ago, leaving him feeling like he lived in a vacuum that could never be filled.

If the death of his last living relative hadn't been enough to make him question his life, seeing a real-life mermaid had. Shaking his head, he reached into his pocket for the shell Magna had given him the day before. Clutching it in his hand, he thought about the strange woman.

The world shifted around him. Ross jerked and his eyes widened when the rope he'd been holding suddenly vanished and the trawler rocked, throwing him off balance and over the side. He only managed a loud curse before he felt the icy cold water surround him.

Ross could swim of course, but the water seemed to be sucking him down. He couldn't break free of the current and reach the surface.

I don't want to die, Ross thought as he was pulled down into the inky blackness.

Find the full book at your favorite distributor with the link below!
books2read.com/themagicshell

ADDITIONAL BOOKS

If you loved this story by me (S.E. Smith) please leave a review! You can discover additional books at: http://sesmithfl.com and http://sesmithya.com or find your favorite way to keep in touch here: https://sesmithfl.com/contact-me/ Be sure to sign up for my newsletter to hear about new releases!

Recommended Reading Order Lists:

http://sesmithfl.com/reading-list-by-events/

http://sesmithfl.com/reading-list-by-series/

The Series

Science Fiction / Romance

Dragon Lords of Valdier Series

It all started with a king who crashed on Earth, desperately hurt. He inadvertently discovered a species that would save his own.

Curizan Warrior Series

The Curizans have a secret, kept even from their closest allies, but even they are not immune to the draw of a little known species from an isolated planet called Earth.

Marastin Dow Warriors Series

The Marastin Dow are reviled and feared for their ruthlessness, but not all want to live a life of murder. Some wait for just the right time to escape….

Sarafin Warriors Series

A hilariously ridiculous human family who happen to be quite formidable… and a secret hidden on Earth. The origin of the Sarafin species is more than it seems. Those cat-shifting aliens won't know what hit them!

Dragonlings of Valdier Novellas

The Valdier, Sarafin, and Curizan Lords had children who just cannot stop getting into trouble! There is nothing as cute or funny as magical, shapeshifting kids, and nothing as heartwarming as family.

Cosmos' Gateway Series

Cosmos created a portal between his lab and the warriors of Prime. Discover new worlds, new species, and outrageous adventures as secrets are unravelled and bridges are crossed.

The Alliance Series

When Earth received its first visitors from space, the planet was thrown into a panicked chaos. The Trivators came to bring Earth into the Alliance of Star Systems, but now they must take control to prevent the humans from destroying themselves. No one was prepared for how the humans will affect the Trivators, though, starting with a family of three sisters....

Lords of Kassis Series

It began with a random abduction and a stowaway, and yet, somehow, the Kassisans knew the humans were coming long before now. The fate of more than one world hangs in the balance, and time is not always linear....

Zion Warriors Series

Time travel, epic heroics, and love beyond measure. Sci-fi adventures with heart and soul, laughter, and awe-inspiring discovery...

Paranormal / Fantasy / Romance

Magic, New Mexico Series

Within New Mexico is a small town named Magic, an... unusual town, to say the least. With no beginning and no end, spanning genres, authors, and universes, hilarity and drama combine to keep you on the edge of your seat!

Spirit Pass Series

There is a physical connection between two times. Follow the stories of those who travel back and forth. These westerns are as wild as they come!

Second Chance Series

Stand-alone worlds featuring a woman who remembers her own death. Fiery and mysterious, these books will steal your heart.

More Than Human Series

Long ago there was a war on Earth between shifters and humans. Humans lost, and today they know they will become extinct if something is not done....

The Fairy Tale Series

A twist on your favorite fairy tales!

A Seven Kingdoms Tale

Long ago, a strange entity came to the Seven Kingdoms to conquer and feed on their life force. It found a host, and she battled it within her body for centuries while destruction and devastation surrounded her. Our story begins when the end is near, and a portal is opened....

Epic Science Fiction / Action Adventure

Project Gliese 581G Series

An international team leave Earth to investigate a mysterious object in our solar system that was clearly made by someone, someone who isn't from Earth. Discover new worlds and conflicts in a sci-fi adventure sure to become your favorite!

New Adult / Young Adult

Breaking Free Series

A journey that will challenge everything she has ever believed about herself as danger reveals itself in sudden, heart-stopping moments.

The Dust Series

Fragments of a comet hit Earth, and Dust wakes to discover the world as he knew it is gone. It isn't the only thing that has changed, though, so has Dust...

ABOUT THE AUTHOR

S.E. Smith is an *internationally acclaimed, New York Times* **and** *USA TODAY Bestselling* author of science fiction, romance, fantasy, paranormal, and contemporary works for adults, young adults, and children. She enjoys writing a wide variety of genres that pull her readers into worlds that take them away.

Printed in Great Britain
by Amazon